P9-BYS-957

TALES
OF THE NOT
FORGOTTEN

TALES
OF
THE NOT
FORGOTTEN

BETH GUCKENBERGER

WARNING: THESE STORIES MAY CHANGE THE WAY YOU SEE THE WORLD

Standard®
P U B L I S H I N G

Cincinnati, Ohio

Published by Standard Publishing, Cincinnati, Ohio
www.standardpub.com

Copyright © 2012 Beth Guckenberger

All rights reserved. No part of this book may be reproduced in any form, except for brief quotations in reviews, without the written permission of the publisher.

These stories are inspired by true events and real people. In some cases, names were changed to protect identities and details of dialogue and actions were imagined. Six billion stories are unfolding daily. These are just a few.

Also available: *Tales of the Not Forgotten Leader's Guide*, 978-0-7847-3527-5.

Printed in: United States of America
Acquisitions editor: Dale Reeves
Project editor: Laura Derico
Cover design and illustration: Scott Ryan
Interior design: Brigid Naglich and Ahaa Design

Portions of "Joel's Hunger" were previously published within *Reckless Faith* (Zondervan).

All Scripture quotations, unless otherwise indicated, are taken from the *HOLY BIBLE, NEW INTERNATIONAL VERSION®. NIV®*. Copyright © 1973, 1978, 1984, 2011 by Biblica, Inc.™ Used by permission. All rights reserved worldwide. Scripture quotations marked (*NASB®*) are taken from the *New American Standard Bible®*. Copyright © 1960, 1962, 1963, 1968, 1971, 1972, 1973, 1975, 1977, 1995 by The Lockman Foundation. Used by permission. (www.Lockman.org) All rights reserved. Scripture quotations marked (*The Message*) are taken from *The Message*. Copyright © by Eugene H. Peterson 1993, 1994, 1995, 1996, 2000, 2001, 2002. Used by permission of NavPress Publishing Group.

ISBN 978-0-7847-3528-2

Library of Congress Cataloging-in-Publication Data

Guckenberger, Beth, 1972-
Tales of the not forgotten / Beth Guckenberger.
v. cm.
Summary: A collection of fictionalized stories based on the real lives of four children in Mexico, Haiti, Nigeria, and India as they intersect with Christian missionaries who seek to help them as they were called by God, the Storyweaver, to do. Includes facts about each country and the issues faced there.
Contents: Introduction: the Storyweaver -- Joel's dinner: how should I pray? -- Seraphina's choice: what can I give? -- Ibrahim's water: where can I go? -- Christiana's mission: who can I serve? -- Epilogue: the pages that came before.
ISBN 978-0-7847-3528-2
[1. Christian life--Fiction. 2. Missionaries--Fiction. 3. Orphans--Fiction.] I. Title.
PZ7.G93463Tal 2012
[Fic]--dc23
2011044550

17 16 15 14 13 12   2 3 4 5 6 7 8 9

To the children who call me
Mom, Mamá, Aunt, and Tía:
I love being in the front row
of your stories.

I will not forget you!
See, I have engraved you
on the palms of my hands.
—Isaiah 49:15, 16

CONTENTS

INTRODUCTION
THE STORY WEAVER

*All the days ordained for me were written in your book
before one of them came to be.*

—Psalm 139:16

He knows you. He has always known you. He knew where you were going to be born, to whom you would be born, and which lives he would weave you into. He's writing your story even now.

God is the Storyweaver.

I know this because he's writing my story too.

My name is Beth, and I live and work as a full-time missionary in Mexico, helping to take care of orphaned children and the people who care for them. All of the stories in this book were inspired by the lives of real people I know, or who have in some way been a part of the ministry I serve, which reaches out to people not only in Mexico, but also in Haiti, Nigeria, and India.

This job I have now wasn't all my idea—there were threads leading me here all along the way.

The first time I remember hearing about a missionary was from my mom. She and my dad had a good friend, Susie Berlemann, who ministered in Asia. Susie would travel home once a year and bring me Barbie clothes from the Philippines. I would wonder what it looked like where Susie lived.

I went to a church with a cool basement, and one year during Vacation Bible School, the VBS teachers made what seemed like a life-size airplane in the basement. We were given plane tickets to go inside—we learned "Cristo Te Amo" that day.

I went on mission trips and read missionary biographies. I had great-grandparents who were pastors and cousins who served in countries with names I couldn't pronounce.

I also loved bike rides and my two brothers, my dad's convertible and eating ice cream. I had a best friend and a swimming pool and . . . no idea I would one day spend years away from it all.

This is my story. And it's just beginning.

Yours is too! Only our Storyweaver knows how he will use your gifts and prayers, where he will send you, and who you will meet on the way. It's certain to be a great adventure!

All great adventures have moments of conflict and suspense. Don't be discouraged. Just hold on and trust—not in what you can see, but in the one who holds it all in his hands.

You'll have so many questions on your journey, starting with: "Do I sit back or go ahead?" You'll have choices to make: "Should I speak up for those who can't or stay silent because I don't know who's listening?" You'll have times of indecision and doubt: "Does anyone hear me?"

God has answers to all these questions and so many more. If you depend on him, he will whisper his answers to your heart—through his Word and through your time spent with him. He will lead you to the places you should go.

He will write your story. And I can't wait to hear it.

Chapter 1
JOEL'S HUNGER

We were out of projects, out of supplies, and out of motivation. And now, we were almost out of time.

Todd and I (Beth) were sponsors for our church's youth mission trip to Querétaro, Mexico. We'd visited there a few years in a row, and we knew in general what to expect. A little paint and polish, some late-night tacos, a little talking to others about Jesus.

The truth was, no one really seemed to care we were there. As I was unpacking the painting materials, I remember thinking, *Haven't we painted this wall before?* We were frustrated, the students on the trip were uninspired, and worst of all, the people we had traveled all this way to serve seemed, well . . . uninterested.

"About two more hours, and we can clean up here and head for dinner," one of the men on our trip came to tell us.

"Two hours, huh?" I sighed and closed my eyes, racking my brain to think of what we could do with two hours. I was just sitting there like that when Todd interrupted my thoughts.

"Do you remember the orphanage we visited in Tirana?" he asked. He had his back to me, bending over as he cleaned some paintbrushes.

My mind flew to another country and another time—another mission trip, one to eastern Europe. I remembered talking to college students about Jesus—it was the first time those young Albanians had ever heard about him! Then one afternoon, someone took us to visit an orphanage . . . "Do I remember? Yes, of course I remember. Why?"

"Do you think there are any orphanages in this town?" He stood up and turned around, but I was already gone. I had run over to where our teens were talking to some of their Mexican counterparts.

"Orphanage-o? Orphanatorio? Orphanagorio?" I tried saying every version of the word I could think of with my best Mexican accent. "*Aqui?*"

"Si, si." They looked at me and laughed, either because the answer was obvious, or because of my funny words. I never found out which.

I ran back over to Todd. We didn't sit down and make a plan. We didn't really think much at all. Within ten minutes of his question, we left the students with the other adult sponsors and jumped into a taxi, feeling like God was leading us to find an orphanage.

Looking back now, it seems so foolish. Silly, even. Right? We didn't really speak Spanish, we didn't have

POST CARD

CORRE SPONDENCE

Spanish is the primary language of people who live in Mexico and many Central and South American countries. Five hundred million people speak Spanish around the world. It is the second most natively spoken language in the world after Mandarin Chinese.

Aqui means "here."

that much money with us if we came into trouble, and we were in a city we could have easily gotten lost in. We should have just stayed with our group, stayed safe.

But an hour later, we landed in front of a children's home on a dusty road and knocked at the door, waving good-bye to our taxi driver.

As we were arguing about who was going to try to talk first, we heard a sound behind the door. Locks being opened. Many locks. *Are they trying to keep*

someone in, I wondered, *or trying to keep someone out?* The door swung open. A man was sitting in a wheelchair, but he seemed eight feet tall. While he waited for us to say something, I tried to look over his shoulder. *Was there a child we could see?*

Todd stumbled through some half remembered high school Spanish phrases, and out of pity I guess, the man let us in the front door. As we rounded the corner, the children came into view. They stared at us with questions on their faces.

I was instantly enchanted. I am sure we, on the other hand, were quite a sight—we still had our painting clothes on from earlier, and we looked and seemed different from anyone in the room.

More than an hour passed, and we were still struggling with our bad Spanish, not getting very far with anyone. Frustrated, Todd got up and started playing basketball with some of the boys, leaving me to plod through my conversation with Mr. Friendly. The stern-looking man and I watched Todd for a while in silence—him with his skeptical look on his face and me, inside still hoping that we were on some kind of holy mission.

The thought crossed my mind that this man maybe had already asked us to leave, and we just didn't understand him. *Was this something you planned, Lord, or are we just in the way?* Then all of a sudden, he turned to me and simply said, "I can understand you. I am an American."

I should have been mad, but I was just relieved! Now we could actually talk.

He continued, "I am a war veteran, and I came to work with abandoned children because I know what it means to be tossed aside. I, like them, am also trying to forget the people who failed me."

I looked at him and said nothing. I silently begged God to help us communicate whatever the reason was that he had led us to this place.

Todd walked over from the court, with the ball under his arm. He had seen us talking, and realized the man could speak English. "We have $200, twenty-five students, and one day left on our trip. What could you do with those resources?" Todd asked. "Is there anything we could do for you if we come tomorrow and help out in some way?"

The man shifted his eyes back and forth and then said softly, "The children haven't had meat in a year, and that window up there is broken." He waved in the direction of a window above us.

And as simple as that, our first mission began.

REMEMBER THIS

War veterans, former soldiers who have served their country in battle, sometimes find it hard to fit back into civilian life once they return from war. Though they should be honored and remembered for their service, some feel forgotten, because people often want to forget hard things such as wars. Have you ever felt like what you did has been forgotten?

The next day, with a clearer sense of where we were headed, we set out for the children's home. On the way, we stopped at a market and bought some

From Beth's Journal

All mission opportunities start like this—looking at what we have in our hands and asking who needs it, then figuring out the best way to build a bridge between the two. Some days all I have is a listening ear, but this day I had some students, pocket change, and a whole day to serve.

toys for the children. When we got to the front door, the children were waiting, laughing and asking if "Michael Jordan" had come back.

We had about 200 hamburgers to grill, a new window, and our students, and we were hoping that by spending the day there, we might do some good.

After some time, Todd finished working on the window and came over to watch me serve some hamburgers. Leaning against the doorframe, he pointed to a preschooler with her hair all tied up and her cheeks smudged with ketchup. "Do you see that little girl?"

"I honestly can't keep my eyes off her—she is precious," I answered, while still managing the grill.

"Well, I think you must've at some point for a minute or two—this is her

$200 in Mexico can buy 200 hamburgers. $1 = 1 hamburger.

fifth time in line, and I don't know any preschooler who can eat that much! I was hoping we could leave enough food for another meal or two. Why don't you follow her and see where the burgers are going?"

This home was built like a bull-fighting arena, with steep stairs, dorms in a circle around the top layer, and a center courtyard where the meal was being served. I went with the girl, her hand in mine, and I could feel her leading me, wanting me to see something.

When we reached the top, she hesitated slightly, then took me to her room. I stood in the doorway and gasped.

The preschoolers were helping each other lift their mattresses and were hiding the meat underneath.

When I walked into the room, I startled them. One of the girls started to cry. What did she think I was going to do? Be mad? Yell? Hit? Take the burgers back? I don't know, but none of that was going through my mind. I just wanted to lift the mattress for the little girl I followed up the stairs, so it wouldn't be so heavy for her.

I wondered about the director of the home and whether he knew what they were doing. After we had carefully hidden the little girl's hamburger, I took her hand and we started out the door. I then stopped and sent her to get Todd.

He came bounding up the stairs, and we stood together, watching the little girls. Something happened to us then. I didn't know it at the time, but now, when I look at the story of my life, I can trace all the events that followed back to that moment in the doorway, watching those girls hide their treasures that had cost us so little.

We walked slowly down the stairs, asking ourselves out loud who we knew who could buy them more hamburgers. When we reached the bottom, I saw the director. He was watching us, waiting for our reaction. He sheepishly explained that he knew the children were saving the hamburgers for later. None of the three of us had the heart to stop them.

The day after the hamburger incident, we flew home. We went back to work. I shopped at the grocery store and called my friends. All the normal things. But something was different.

It was as if there were a big wooden marker in the shape of an arrow pointing to somewhere I couldn't see, but a place I was nervous about and excited to explore. The path I was on that had seemed fine just a

God promises orphans that he will . . .

hear them (Exodus 22:22, 23).

defend their cause (Deuteronomy 10:18; Psalm 82:3).

give them food and clothing (Deuteronomy 10:18; 14:29).

be their helper (Psalm 10:14).

vindicate them (Psalm 10:18, NASB).

not leave them (Psalm 27:10; Jeremiah 49:11).

be their Father (Psalm 68:5).

give them a home (Psalm 68:6).

rescue them (Psalm 82:4).

deliver them (Psalm 82:4).

lift them up (Psalm 113:7).

secure justice for them (Psalm 140:12).

uphold their cause (Psalm 140:12).

not forget them (Isaiah 49:15).

give them compassion (Hosea 14:3).

lead them out (John 10:3).

come to them (John 14:18).

week before, now looked—in light of my recent experience—just OK. And I didn't want OK anymore. So I moved around for about a year, trying to get comfortable again, but there was that arrow, always pointing me back to that afternoon in Mexico.

Today, when people look at our ministry and ask about strategy and planning, we smile inside. It's tempting to try to make it seem like we've planned out every step and always knew where we were going.

But the truth is, it all started with a little girl hiding a hamburger under her mattress.

One August, I was speaking at Grace Chapel, a church in Cincinnati, Ohio, about Back2Back Ministries and God's promises to orphans. When I was finished, I stood chatting with some of the members of the church. A man came up to me and said, "Monterrey—that's where you live? I know that city. I travel there on business regularly." He handed me his business card and asked for one of mine. "The next time I'm in town, I will call you and take your family out to dinner, and then you can show me the children's homes."

"Sounds great," I said. I handed him my card, but I confess, I was distracted. Other people were passing by, my skirt had no pockets, and in the confusion, I lost his card.

One of my children tugged at my skirt. "I'm hungry. Can we go now?"

"OK, baby." And with that, my thoughts turned toward where we would go for lunch.

Boys at Edgar's children's home help organize supplies.

"I'm hungry!" The cries for more food were ringing in Edgar's ears. He heard those words from more than fifty different voices every day at the children's home. He was the director. He wanted to provide for all the children. But it was November—it was starting to get cold. He needed to pay for heat. And he was running out of money—the people who used to give money to the home had stopped giving. It was a hard time for everyone.

As the sun rose that morning, the light shining through a gate created shadow bars across the hallway where Edgar was walking. He was reminded of the story of Joseph in prison that he had taught some of the children not long ago. How God had not forgotten Joseph, even though others did, and how Joseph eventually became God's tool to save thousands of people from starving.

"Should we use our remaining money for heat, blankets, or food?" Edgar wondered aloud.

It costs about $100 per month to care for a child in an orphanage. Many aid organizations offer ways to sponsor a child.

Edgar could have picked up the phone and called us. Our ministry would have brought some food over for the evening meal—an emergency kit of beans and rice, and eggs and oil and tortillas. But something in his heart knew that neither he nor the children should feel dependent on people. It wasn't

Every good and perfect gift is from above, coming down from the Father of the heavenly lights, who does not change like shifting shadows.

—James 1:17

pride that stopped him that day from calling us, but more of a fear that the children were putting people on a pedestal fit only for the King—the giver of all good gifts.

He spent the remaining money that Saturday morning on an *almuerzo*. The kids filled up and asked for more. Edgar sat back and prayed throughout the day, knowing there was no more food, and no more pesos, and dozens of children whose stomachs would be grumbling again within a few more hours.

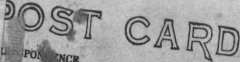

POST CARD

CORRESPONDENCE

An almuerzo is a brunch-like meal, usually consisting of an egg or meat dish. In this case, Edgar had no meat for the children.

An almuerzo is "brunch."

I answered the phone on a fall Saturday afternoon. "Beth?" The voice on the other end didn't sound familiar. "It's me—Carlos. Remember? Grace Chapel? Ohio?"

Oh yeah . . . what did I do with that card he gave me? "Hola, Carlos! How are you doing? Are you here in Monterrey?"

"I am! And I will be done with business around six o'clock—are you free tonight? If so, why don't you come pick me up and we can grab some dinner. Then you can show me around some of the orphanages you serve."

I thought through our evening plans. *Where you go, I will follow,* I breathed. "Just tell us when and where and we'll be there."

After making some plans, we hung up.

The afternoon rolled on and it was nearing the next mealtime. His own stomach growling, Edgar knew it was time to ask God—together with the children—for what he had planned for them. Saying a silent prayer, he stood up and called for the children to join him in the *comedor*.

> There are approximately 10 million orphans in Mexico.

The kids gathered around the table, curious why there weren't any plates set out. Edgar started, "We don't have anything to eat for dinner tonight." One of the youngest, a boy named Joel, looked around with big eyes, checking to see if anyone else thought *Tio* Edgar might be joking. He continued, "But this is what we know—you are the children of the Most High King and you are not forgotten. So let's pray and ask the King for your dinner."

POST CARD

CORRESPONDENCE

Comedor means "dining room."

"Dear Lord, we thank you for your numerous blessings on these children and on this home. We humbly ask that you would provide a meal for us tonight . . ." And on he went, when suddenly he was interrupted by Joel.

"Tio," he started out slowly, "are you serious? Are we really praying for God to bring us dinner?" Joel looked at him incredulously. "What kind of food does *God* deliver?"

Edgar, always looking for a moment to teach the children, seized this chance. "Joel, God loves you and you are his child. Yes, we are asking him for your dinner. He's your Father and he wants you to know he sees you. It's his pleasure to want to lavish his riches on you. It is he who owns the cattle on a thousand hills—every part of creation belongs to him. So let's just see what he will deliver to us."

Every animal of the forest is mine, and the cattle on a thousand hills. I know every bird in the mountains, and the insects in the fields are mine. If I were hungry I would not tell you, for the world is mine, and all that is in it.
—Psalm 50:10-12

They bowed their heads and all began to pray again, when Joel, unable to sit still through this prayer, interrupted Edgar once more. "Do you think . . . will the Lord bring us . . . *meat?*"

To a boy whose diet was mainly beans and rice, tortillas and hot dogs, real meat seemed like a mighty request. Edgar took a deep breath—fifty pairs of eyes were on him. "You can ask for anything in the Lord's name."

So they bowed their heads again, praying for dinner and meat in Jesus' name. But while the other heads were still bowed, Joel shoved his hand into the air, not able to stand it any longer, and asked, "Tio, what *kind* of meat does God bring you? What can I ask for? How do I pray?"

POST CARD

Tio means "uncle."

The phone was ringing again. This time when I answered, I recognized the voice. "Beth? It's Carlos. Hey, do you have a pickup truck you can bring tonight?"

I was picturing the three of us in the truck cab, squeezed together in the front seat, when I answered slowly, "Ye-s, we have a truck. Why would we need to use that?"

"Oh, I just thought you might want some of my leftover product. Do you? It's been here all day and I can't fly it back over the border. People are already starting to throw it out in the dumpsters in the back. But I was thinking about your kids. Do you want any of it? Could you use it?"

Uh-oh. Time to confess!

"Carlos, I hate to admit this, but I misplaced your business card. What kind of 'product' are we talking about?"

"Oh, Beth," he laughed at me. "Remember? I represent the meat company. We are here at a big meat convention, trying to attract some new restaurant business. All my orders have been placed, and now I'm just going to discard the samples, which have been thawing all day. There are lots of others here selling, like me. Can you use some meat if I round it up?"

"Of course, Carlos! Thanks for thinking of us. We have lots of mouths to feed. We'll bring the truck and pick you up in a couple of hours."

Todd decided to head over early and called me an hour later. "Beth, there's so much meat we've collected, I'm using tie-down straps in the back. It's way too much for us to store in the deep freezer; we'll need to drop this off tonight at the homes. I'm going to start unloading it at some of the children's homes located here downtown on the way to the restaurant. Will you call ahead for me?"

Joel's home was the first one on his route.

When I called the children's home to report on the coming food donation, Edgar seemed strangely not surprised.

"Hey Edgar, it's Beth. I just wanted to check and see if you were home. Todd is on his way over with a food donation for you."

There was a pause on the other end of the phone. "Beth, do you know what kind of donation it is?" Edgar asked calmly.

Monterrey, Mexico, is a city of around 8 million people, located about 150 miles from Texas.

"It's some kind of meat," I answered. "I'm not totally sure of all the details. Just wanted to make sure you would be around."

"You don't know anything about it?"

A bit exasperated, I tried to get off the phone—I had several other calls to make. "Edgar, I know he wanted me to check and see if you had room in your freezer. Do you?"

"Yes, I do. But would you mind terribly finding out what kind of meat it is and then calling us back?" he asked hesitantly.

"What do you mean, 'What kind of meat'? It's meat, Edgar—it's *food*. Why should it matter?"

"Well, Beth, it does matter. Would you mind calling me back when you know?"

Todd was already on his way, carefully navigating the streets, making sure not to lose any of the precious cargo in the back of the truck. I didn't want to bother him, but Edgar had sounded so strange, and I had in fact told him I would ask. So I called. "Todd, this is kind of an odd question, but do you know what *kind* of meat it is? I don't know when we got so picky, but Edgar wants to know."

"Beth, you won't believe it! It's the best meat money can buy—steak and incredible cuts of beef and pork. There's filet mignon, sirloin, New York strip . . . The sellers here had put out these amazing samples to attract new buyers. The homes are going to love it."

"Praise God!" Edgar breathed into the phone, after hearing my report about the

Pesos are the Mexican form of dollars. The general minimum wage in Mexico is around 57 pesos a day, which is a little over $4.

meat. I couldn't help but notice how relieved he sounded. He asked me to hold for a moment. He was covering the phone, but I could easily hear him shouting out to someone, "God is on his way over with your meat!"

There was an explosion of voices—the children, erupting into cheers. I wondered what all the noise was about. It was almost as if they had been planning to have a party.

Edgar got back on the phone. "Oh, Beth, remember this day, *we are not forgotten*!"

It wasn't until later that I heard the whole story, about how they had run out of food earlier in the day. About the celebration that night in their house, and how it kept the kids up past their usual bedtime. About the wonderful dinner they had, and how delicious the food was. About the thanks they gave for the King who owns the cattle on a thousand hills and was generous enough to share the best of what he had with his children.

And about four-year-old Joel and his hunger for answers.

 Those children prayed that day with the faith of a mustard seed. (Do you know what the faith of a four-year-old orphan looks like? It's pretty small.) They prayed, and the mountain moved. And it's still moving.

I moved that night too, wrestling, like Joel, with my faith. Most days, when I see a risk coming, I get out of the way. I angle myself so I don't get anywhere near it. I stay safe. I don't let myself get pushed into a place where I have to cry out for my Rescuer.

But I'm learning. I want to say the things I've held back, take the risks I've been dying to take. I want to go to the places where I'm not sure how to get out, so I can be grateful when God shows up to guide me. I want to learn more about how his ways are not like mine.

I want to ask more questions. I want to pray more for things I can't see.

REMEMBER THIS

How do you pray? Do you pray for things that are within your reach? Or do you ever ask God for things that are bigger than anything you could ever do? Jesus said that if you have faith as small as a mustard seed, you can tell a mountain to move and it will move (Matthew 17:20). How might his words change the way you pray?

When I find myself in a difficult position, like the kind Edgar purposely put himself in, my tendency is to call out to people first, instead of God. And do you know what you get when you call out to people?

You get beans and rice and eggs and oil and tortillas—which at first seems filling, but actually, it's pretty cheap.

With God, you get steak.

In Matthew 17:20, Jesus said, "Truly I tell you, if you have faith as small as a mustard seed, you can say to this mountain, 'Move from here to there,' and it will move. Nothing will be impossible for you." What are some "mountains" (problems, difficult challenges) you would like to see moved in your life? What do you think Jesus meant when he said, "Nothing will be impossible for you"? Write your thoughts about the story of Joel here.

Chapter 2

SERAPHINA'S CHOICE

"*Sè*, where are you?" Genevieve rolled over and felt her sister Seraphina's arm tucking around her. Muttering contentedly, she fell back asleep.

But now Seraphina was awake. She lay there, staring at the makeshift cardboard roof of their tent, and her mind began to spin. *Is that rain again?* She pictured how muddy the dump would be. *What will I find for us to eat today? Jesus, can you hear me? Do you see us? Have you forgotten us?*

"Us" meant Seraphina and her five-year-old twin sisters. "Us" used to include their mother, but on

POST CARD

CORRESPONDENCE

Haiti has two official languages: French and Haitian Creole. Seraphina and her sisters speak Creole.

Sè means "sister" in Creole.

another rainy day a couple of years ago, not long after Seraphina's seventh birthday, she left for her job in the rice fields and never came back. Seraphina once worried about her a lot, but not much anymore. She had other things to worry about now.

Her other sister, Nadia, whimpered with her eyes closed tight, as if she was having a bad dream. Seraphina smoothed Nadia's forehead gently and whispered to her the words her mother used to say to them as they were falling asleep beside her: "Whoever dwells in the shelter of the Most High will rest in the shadow of the Almighty" (Psalm 91:1). It was one of the few things she still remembered about her mother. Then she would say *bon nuit* and kiss their foreheads.

POST CARD

PON NCE

Bon nuit means "good night."

Seraphina hoped her mother was resting somewhere nice tonight.

When the first light of morning came, Seraphina
got up and gathered her bags. She kissed her sisters
and told them, "Stay in the tent. Stay together. And—"

"Stay safe!" the twins finished in unison. They
knew the routine. Seraphina said they were too little
yet to make the difficult trek to the dump, so they
remained behind every day while she went looking
for food for them. As she started out, she prayed, as
she always did, to the One who could look after them.

She hated leaving them behind on their own, but
she didn't want them at the dump either. And besides,
they could never make that long walk—it was a
couple of kilometers—and she had no wagon to carry
them when they got tired.

This morning, Seraphina was tired too, after
getting so little sleep the night before. But she pressed

on, picking her way through the muddy roads and jumping over ditches until the mountains of freshly dumped loads came into sight. Of course, she could smell the place long before she saw it—a burnt, rotten odor hung in the air. Little fires had been built every twenty-five steps or so, burning down the trash everyone had already picked over.

2 kilometers = 1.2 miles = about 24 laps around a high school basketball court.

She joined the hundreds of other people crawling all over the mounds, like beetles, scavenging for bits of food—maybe a discarded bag of wet rice, crusts of old bread, or partially eaten fruit. Whenever something fresh or good was found, the finder scurried away, anxious to hide the treasure before someone else could get it.

A dog sniffed at Seraphina's feet and then slinked off. Seraphina had learned to remain still when any animals were close to her. The lesson had come the hard way, and she instinctively rubbed the pinkish scar on her brown arm where she had been bitten a few months ago. The animals were as desperate to find food as the people. Some people even tried to trap the pigs, dogs, and other wild animals that roamed the dump. Anything for fresh meat.

Seraphina's sharp eyes scanned each foot of garbage she walked over, watching not just for food, but for scraps of metal or plastics that could be sold, traded, or recycled. Whenever she found more than

they needed, she would trade the extra for clothes others had found. Some days there were treasures; other days it was hard to beat the competition. She knew the faces of most of the kids who came to the dump, but not all of their names. Most traveled in small packs, staying with their brothers or sisters or cousins.

Without any siblings old enough to accompany her, Seraphina stayed on her own most of the time. It suited her. As she moved slowly over the heaps, she made up stories in her head about all sorts of things: stories about the other children she saw, stories of where her mother might be, stories about where she might one day go. It helped her pass the time while she waited for another truck to dump some fresh garbage.

Sometimes Seraphina dreamed of going to

school—she knew some kids her age went there. On one of her first trips to the dump, she had gotten turned around on her way back to the tent. She'd ended up on a street where there was a school. Peering in one of the windows, she'd seen a whole room filled with books. She wondered what kinds of stories were inside them all. She could read very few words on her own, and she longed to know more. But she knew school could not be part of her life right now.

Before the sun was too low in the sky, Seraphina repositioned her bags on her shoulders and headed home. "Alo sè," she greeted the twins, as she reached their tent and the little girls came running out.

"It was getting very dark," Genevieve whined.

Seraphina pointed at the horizon. "The clouds are hiding the sun, but it hasn't gone to bed yet, see?" She ran her hand over the child's fuzzy braids. "You know I always make it home before dark."

She tried to make the nights fun for the three of them, acting out the stories she had composed in her head that day, or ones she had heard long ago. The dump provided the props: a small plastic bottle became an airplane, a broken lamp was a sword, a torn basket could be a treasure chest.

The little plays served as a good distraction for the twins when there wasn't enough food for a meal and their stomachs complained. Even though there were no pages or pictures, Seraphina's imagination was as thick as the humidity hanging in the air. In this make-believe world, help was always on the way, no matter what dangerous situation they pretended to be in.

Giggles poured out of the tent as Seraphina finished acting out a scene where a very mean and stingy king piled up his riches so high that they ended up falling on him and trapping him in his very own castle.

"Another one!" Nadia begged, clapping her hands.

Seraphina shook her head. "No, no. It is too late—we all need to sleep. Besides, if you close your eyes, in your head is a giant storybook, and you can live out whatever stories you want."

"Please, please, sè! Tell us the one about the boy and his lunch basket that fed a whole city! Pleeeeease?"

Seraphina couldn't resist. She loved most to tell the stories of the great Storyweaver—stories she half remembered from her mother, and from a church man who visited the dump one week each month.

"All right, then. Sit up, you two, and listen. One day the man named Jesus walked up a mountain and sat down with his friends . . . "

"*Please sit up* and put away your tray tables," the flight attendant's voice crackled over the airplane speakers. "We will be landing in Port-au-Prince in a few minutes."

Brian looked out the window at the glimpses he could get through the clouds of the green and brown island below. It already seemed so different to him, even from way up here. Since he'd first heard about the mission trip, he'd known he wanted to come. The timing had been difficult—it seemed like something had fallen apart every moment leading up to his getting on the plane. But in the end, conflicts were resolved and the money was gathered and . . . now what?

The beauty and devastation of the Haitian landscape came into focus with one long stare. He sighed and leaned back. *What am I doing here, Lord? I know I wanted to see and serve another part of the world, but I don't even know what I have to offer.* He pressed his hands against his eyes. *I don't even know what I believe you have to offer.*

It had been a hard couple of months leading up to the trip, and doubts had nestled into Brian's heart about how and when God would act in the stories of lives he had heard about. Or in his own.

I just don't know about this, God. He closed his eyes and imagined for a moment he was somewhere else, anywhere else but here.

I don't know about this. Seraphina looked out from under the plastic bag hood she had made for herself. It had been raining all night and all morning. She fell in line behind the other children, making their way barefoot to the dump. The other kids were loud, singing and pushing each other into puddles. But Seraphina couldn't help but worry. *Will there be enough for all of us?*

She escaped into her thoughts, humming a silly song her mom had once taught her about a whale and a mermaid. She couldn't remember every word, and made up the parts she forgot. *LaSiren, LaBalenn . . .*

HAITI

Port au-Prince

Port-au-Prince is the capital and the largest city in Haiti.

Riding in the back of a *tap-tap*, Brian was lost in thought. They were on the way to a dump, he'd been told. So far on this trip he had visited an overcrowded school and a tent church that was spilling over, had toured some of the wreckage from the earthquake and seen more orphanages than he thought his heart could handle.

His head was pounding. *What's the point of all this, Lord? You've brought me here to show me thousands of children living with nothing. And for what? What can I give? How can I possibly help them all? And where are you? What made you think I could make any difference here at all?*

As the rest of the group were laughing and chatting around him, he tried to distract himself by singing the Creole song they had learned that morning in church. He couldn't remember every word, and made up the parts he forgot.

When she arrived at the dump, she saw a white man walking around, with broad shoulders and clean clothes. She noticed his baseball hat—she'd uncovered one of those here a few weeks ago and traded it for some bread a boy had. The man didn't have any bags for carrying treasures and he wasn't picking anything up.

The earthquake that hit Haiti on January 12, 2010, caused at least $14 billion of damage to a country that was already struggling. Before the earthquake 78 percent of Haitians were considered poor, having an income of less than $2 a day. And 54 percent lived in extreme poverty (less than $1 a day).

But when he turned toward her, Seraphina spotted the camera hanging around his neck. *Hmm. Maybe one of those news people, here to take pictures of us.* Photographers had been all over the place that year.

POST CARD

CORRESPONDENCE

A tap-tap is a kind of public transportation in Haiti. It is usually a kind of pickup truck with seats and a hood.

LaSiren, LaBalenn,
Chapo'm tonbe nan la me.
LaSiren, LaBalenn,
Chapo'm tonbe nan la me.

The Siren, the Whale,
My hat falls into the sea.
The Siren, the Whale,
My hat falls into the sea.

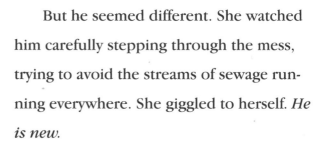

But he seemed different. She watched him carefully stepping through the mess, trying to avoid the streams of sewage running everywhere. She giggled to herself. *He is new.*

She continued to watch him from a safe distance, staying behind a broken refrigerator. He was just taking pictures and looking around. Then he lowered the camera and wiped his eyes.

Seraphina followed his every move, and when he reached into his pocket, she inched forward, straining to see what he had in his hand. She was trying to be so quiet. But her foot caught on something sticking up out of the ground, and she fell.

Brian wiped the sweat from his eyes and almost without thinking continued his conversation in his head with God. *I have heard the stories, Lord. I know the answer is bigger than me, bigger than the help I can bring. I know I am hungry as well, broken as well, desperate as well. Maybe not in the same ways as these children, but enough in other ways to know it's complicated. I want to help, not hurt. I want to be inside your adventure, not writing my own. Guide me. I am here at your bidding. Use me.*

He reached into his pocket for a cloth to wipe his camera lens and saw movement out of the corner of his eye. He turned and didn't see anything at first—the landscape was so filled with bits and pieces of garbage, it was hard to focus. But then he saw her—her pigtails sticking up from her head as she raised herself up from the ground. *Oh! It's a little girl! Is she OK?*

In just a few of his long strides he was by her, but she had already made it to her feet. He looked her over to see if she had been hurt by her fall and noticed the bruises and scabs all over her legs. *Probably not the first time she's fallen here,* he thought. When he caught her eye, she smiled shyly at him. *What a beautiful smile!* He couldn't help smiling back at her.

What could I give her? He touched the wrapper of a granola bar in his pocket. He had counted on it being his plan B for lunch. Meals on this trip had been a little unpredictable. *She doesn't look like a girl with a plan B for lunch.*

Seraphina felt suddenly on edge. She'd broken one of her own rules—getting too close to a stranger. This man seemed nice, but . . . Just then he reached into his pocket again and held something out to her. *Maybe a candy bar?* She glanced nervously around. *If others see him, they will make a scene and all come over here.* She considered running away right then, but the man said, "Take it. It's yours." She didn't understand the words he was saying, but she read his body language, and in one swift movement, she

bridged the gap between them and took the bar, shoving it under her shirt as she hurried away.

When she was far enough away to feel safe, she stole a peek at her treasure. She knew what it was now. She remembered when a big trash bag full of them was found in the dump earlier that year and how fast everyone grabbed them. She hadn't  been quick enough that time to get one, but she knew it had to be something good. *Now I can go back early to the girls; they won't have to be alone for so long. What a lucky day!*

Seraphina looked over her shoulder back up to the top of the hill where the man had been standing, but he was gone now. *Who is he? What just happened?*

What just happened? *Who is she, Lord?* Brian slowly made his way back to where the other team members were gathering. He couldn't get the little girl's face out of his head. *I know you know. You see her, you love her. You have not forgotten her. Be with her, whatever her story. Protect her, speak to her . . . give me the chance to tell her the truth about how precious she is, about who you made her to be.*

He had wanted to follow her, but she seemed so startled, he didn't want to scare her more. Later, as they were getting ready to leave the area, he kept an eye out for her, even heading down an unknown path for a while because he thought he caught sight of the back of her head. But she was gone.

That night Brian tossed and turned in his bed, uncomfortable in the heat. He thought of the girl, the dump, his own home . . . He pictured the rows of neat containers he and his neighbors used for their trash. *Wonder how much is in those bins that someone could use.* He imagined what the girl's story might be, filling in the blanks with details he had been learning about Haiti. *Lord, I don't know what you are asking of me. I have more questions than answers. Wherever she is and whoever she is, I just pray you let her know she is seen. By me. By you. Let me have the chance to tell her (and others like her) you see her too.*

Brian kicked the thin sheet off his bed and shook his head in frustration. *Who am I kidding? I don't even know her language—what do I have to offer her?*

At home that night, Seraphina opened the wrapper and shared the granola bar with her sisters. As they

Nearly half the population of Haiti are children under the age of eighteen. There are approximately 490,000 orphans. About 200,000 orphans live in institutions; others are in foster homes, live with relatives, or stay on the streets.

munched on that and the few other bits of food Seraphina had collected in her bags that day, she told them about the man with the sad eyes and the camera. The girls had more questions than their big sister had answers, so she imagined a story.

"There was one day a kind farmer, who went on a journey to find some special plants to grow in his fields. But he wandered too far and lost his way home . . ." Seraphina and the twins started acting out the story. The kind farmer saw the girls playing and asked for help. The girls gave him directions and drew him a map, and he in turn gave them a ride on his wagon. They headed off together toward his homeland . . .

The next day, Seraphina repeated the routine she had known for years now. She woke up, rubbing her face with a little of the water that they caught each day running off the top of the tent and collected in buckets. Then she woke the girls up and told them she would return soon with something to eat, reminding them to stay in the shelter of the tent. She gave them little chores to keep them busy—weaving new bed mats out of the long reeds they had collected, stuffing "pillows" with plastic bags she'd gathered from the dump, and other small tasks to try to keep their home as comfortable as it could be.

Heading to the dump, she walked alongside a girl she had seen several times. She mustered up the courage to ask, "Are you new?"

"I live with my grandmother. We aren't new, but she was the one who used to come and look for our family. She's sick and is getting weak, so now I have taken her place."

Seraphina studied her for a moment, wishing she could see a friend instead of competition. She sighed, "I hope you find what you are looking for today." The

From Beth's Journal

Helping others requires us to look up as we serve. If we look only at those we are serving, we might expect something back they can't give. If we look around, our motives might go wrong or we might compare our giving with that of someone else. When we look up, at Jesus, then our service is really our gift to him—and that is always enough.

girl didn't answer, but grabbed Seraphina's hand. They walked the rest of the long way together, connected.

Seraphina thought about telling her about the man from yesterday. He was on her mind, and she didn't know what else to talk to the girl about. Maybe if she told her about him, they could split up and look for him all over the dump. Could she trust her?

But as they turned the corner, she realized she didn't need to tell her anything. There he was! Her heart skipped a beat.

He was surrounded by children. *Maybe he has more of those bars with him?*

"Who is that?" her new friend

asked. Without even knowing what she was hurrying for, she broke into a trot, pulling Seraphina along with her. "Do you think he has something for us?"

Seraphina was having trouble keeping up—her ankle had been hurting a little ever since her fall yesterday afternoon. The girl said, "I can run faster. I will try to save you a spot in line!"

Seraphina let go of her hand, and the girl ran on ahead, joining the crowd surrounding the man. Her heart fell. More and more children were coming. The secret was out. *He won't even see me in this big crowd. And if he did, would he remember me? What would I say to him? I don't speak his language. God, could you make him understand?*

For a moment she was excited at the idea of making his eyes smile, of thanking him for last night's dinner. She pressed her way into the sprawling line, behind her new friend. But the man was busy and distracted. He looked right over her.

Brian surveyed the growing crowd. *Will we have enough?* The children approached from every direction. Some of them looked hardened; their eyes empty. Others pushed each other around and played like they were in line for recess at elementary school. *I know this isn't the answer forever, Lord. Please make it right for today.*

As he bent down to grab more sandwiches, he caught sight of the girl he had seen the day before. *I wonder if she liked the breakfast bar I gave her.* He tried to make eye contact with her, and he saw her smile and duck behind the teenage girl in front of her. He looked at the people standing by her to see if any of them seemed to be with her. The older girl kept talking to her. *A sister maybe?* But they didn't look very much alike. *What is her story?*

As she came up in the line, he handed her a bologna sandwich and repeated the simple phrase he'd learned this morning and memorized, *"Ou pa bliye."*

Once again, their eyes connected. Seraphina could tell he saw her and knew her—he remembered yesterday too. A hundred thoughts flooded her mind in a moment. She wanted to tell him thanks for the food, for the night of fun with her sisters that he didn't even know he had provided. She wanted to say thank you for a day of not fighting for something to eat, and for the courage it had

Brian lives in Ohio and works full-time for an organization that cares for orphans around the world.

given her to make a new friend today. She glanced over at her "competition" laughing in line and then looked back at the man, willing him to know how

POST CARD

CORRESPONDENCE

Ou pa bliye means "You are not forgotten."

grateful she was for these small bits of relief.

I should give him something. She reached into one of her bags, but she already knew it was empty. *What do I have?* She looked down at her sandwich. It was a large sandwich—big enough to feed her and her sisters tonight. She felt torn, confused.

Then she looked up at the man, giving sandwiches to so many people, and she knew what to do. Ripping the sandwich in half and sneaking up behind him, she tucked a half into one of the giant pockets on the side of his shorts.

POST CARD

CORRESPONDENCE

Mèsi means "thank you."

Feeling a tug at his side, he spun around to look at her, and she froze. Tears sprang into her eyes.

"*Mèsi*," he said softly, reaching down to give her a hug. She trembled. *Lord, why is this girl giving away food? To me?* His heart started pounding and the hairs stood up on the back of his neck. God was whispering something to him.

He groaned inwardly. *I've been here for a week and this little street child is showing me more than I've learned anywhere else. It's not about giving what I'm required to give, and worrying about what I get to keep. It's not about what's fair, or fifty-fifty, or even 10 percent. It's just about what I have in my hand right now, and who I can share it with.*

He held up the half sandwich and grinned at her, and then took a big bite. Her eyes lit up. She looked like he had just given her the best present in the world. *Lord, please fill her heart to overflowing. Please show me what I can give her and others like her.*

He'd had so many questions for God this week. Now he could hear God asking him one.

"Brian, what's your bologna sandwich?"

God loves it when the giver delights in the giving.

God can pour on the blessings in astonishing ways so that you're ready for anything and everything, more than just ready to do what needs to be done. As one psalmist puts it,

> *He throws caution to the winds,*
> *giving to the needy in reckless abandon.*
> *His right-living, right-giving ways*
> *never run out, never wear out.*

This most generous God who gives seed to the farmer that becomes bread for your meals is more than extravagant with you. He gives you something you can then give away, which grows into full-formed lives, robust in God, wealthy in every way, so that you can be generous in every way, producing with us great praise to God.

—2 Corinthians 9:7-11 (*The Message*)

Seraphina laughed and cried and ran all the way home. By the time she saw her home at the end of the dirt road, she had written and rewritten the story in her head over and over again. She couldn't wait to reenact it for her sisters.

When they came running out to meet her this time, she didn't say a thing. She just turned her bag over and dumped out the three wrapped-up sandwiches the man had gathered for her before she left. The girls squealed in surprise. Seraphina laughed and sat down on a mat. She thought about the fourth sandwich she had had—the one she had given to her new friend to take to her grandmother. She smiled again as she remembered the look on the girl's face, and how she had promised to walk with her tomorrow.

As the twins ate happily, Seraphina told them of all her encounters that day. About how she had shared her sandwich with the kind "farmer" and the feeling it had given her. About the look in his eyes and how he had hugged her so tight, just like Mama used to do. About how he had used the few Creole words he knew to find out about her family ("*Frè? Sè? Konbyen?*"), and when he knew she had two sisters, how he had quietly motioned to the other man with

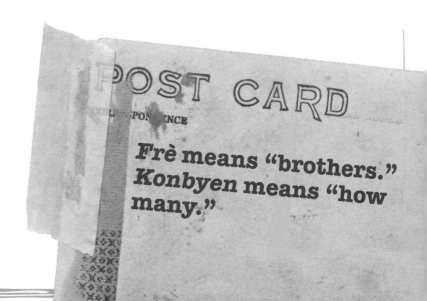

Frè means "brothers." Konbyen means "how many."

him and collected a couple of extra sandwiches for her to take home.

She sat back, for once completely filled up. It had felt so good to be able to give something away! She told her sisters how this giving had made her feel. "I want to do more giving. Tomorrow at the dump, I will look for something I can share, instead of trade."

Genevieve and Nadia looked at her with big eyes. They didn't know exactly what Seraphina was talking about, but they were glad to see her so happy.

They begged her to tell the story again, and this time they joined in: trading parts and making up lines for the man whose words Seraphina could hardly understand, but whose heart she could hear loud and clear: *You are not forgotten.*

As she lay on the floor of the tent that night, snuggled between her two sisters, she stared up at the cardboard roof and her mind was filled with hope. She pictured the muddy dump she would visit the next day. *Jesus, thank you for remembering us. Thank you for the man who saw me. What will be my bologna sandwich tomorrow? I can't wait to see what you will bring me, and what I can give.*

And for the first time, Seraphina felt she was in a story she didn't have to imagine.

REMEMBER THIS

What can you give? Generosity changes everything. The more you share, the more you seem to have. Some days you'll have money to give, other days you'll have time to share. Some days you'll just offer a prayer for someone. When you share whatever you have, you'll find yourself with more than when you started. Every time. We can't out-give God.

Now it's time to use your imagination. Imagine you live in a makeshift tent home, like Seraphina and her sisters. What would you think if you got left there on your own? What would you do? How would you find food?

Does living where you live or having the things you have make you feel safe or happy or comfortable? How much could you give away before you would feel uncomfortable? Write your thoughts about the story of Seraphina here.

Chapter 3
IBRAHIM'S THIRST

The Friday afternoon sun was hot on Ibrahim's bare back as he bent over to help his mother in the fields. Bare back and bare feet—that's the way Ibrahim liked it. Made him feel free.

He stopped to eat a mango as he put several of the ripe, orange fruits in his bag. It tasted so sweet, he couldn't even feel the growing ache in his legs from standing all day.

Uwata *always warns us*, he thought. *If I eat too many, my belly will hurt.*

POST CARD

CORRESPONDENCE

Ibrahim speaks Hausa. There are over forty languages in Nigeria, and most Nigerians speak a tribal language, a school language like Hausa, and English.

Uwata means "my mother."

He threw the rest of his unfinished fruit on the ground.

He saw his sister Esther up ahead. Walking backwards as she chattered to their cousin, she was still too small to hold a bag over her shoulder. She wasn't much help; she just came along for the company, and because she couldn't be left alone yet.

Ibrahim smiled—she could make him laugh even when he was tired. Her exaggerated imitation of the  "aunts" as they carried the water on their heads, swinging their hips side to side, could bust him up every time. Esther didn't know hard work yet. The little girl still thought being in the mango grove was another chance to play. *She'll know soon enough,* he thought.

They had lived here with the aunts for as long as Ibrahim could remember. He had heard the story now so many times, some days he felt like he could picture it—as if he could remember it himself. But he had been too young to remember—just four years old when his mother was kicked out of their home and took him and baby Esther with her in the middle of the night.

The aunts were all sisters (or so they called themselves), but not sisters by birth. Even better, they often said, is being sisters in Christ.

It had all started when one of the aunts, aptly named Endurance, had heard about Jesus while visiting a medical clinic for her injured foot. She'd been run over in the street by a motorcycle. The missionary doctor who helped her in the weeks after the accident invited her to church. One morning, she snuck out to go to the church service. It was against her family's beliefs for her to go to a Christian church. If anyone found out, bad things could happen. But she went anyway. The doctor had been so kind to her, and she wanted to hear more about this man, Jesus, who had died and come to life again.

The country of Nigeria is at least 50 percent Muslim. For many years and still today, violent attacks have been a threat to Nigerians who choose to follow Jesus.

Not long after that, she decided to follow Jesus. Endurance began to quietly tell her friends the stories of Jesus she heard in church, and one by one, as these eight women friends came to know him, they paid a big price. Their families didn't understand why they would walk away from the religion of their ancestors, the Muslim faith.

Over time, when the women refused to stop following Jesus, their families rejected them *and* their new faith. Each of the women had been forced to choose—either leave her home or renounce the God she had just accepted. Their husbands and parents and cousins and neighbors—everyone they knew— stood against them as they walked away and chose the Lord instead.

Ibrahim sat down for a moment in the shade.

The older he became, almost twelve now, the more he realized how hard that must have been for his mother. He couldn't imagine being asked to leave his home—to walk away from everything and everyone he knew.

Sometimes it made him mad just thinking about how she had been treated. *Uwata is a good mother—so strong and so kind to me.* He hoped he could be that brave if God ever asked him to be.

But he felt safe here now. Ibrahim looked off toward the Zagun village, where the huts sat together like old women gathered around a fire. There the aunts had come together with their children and had formed a family of sorts—eight women, one elderly grandmother,

and twenty-six children, all living together, leaning on each other, protecting one another.

He glanced up, judging how much of the day was left by how low the sun was sitting in the sky. *Soon,* he thought, *the call will come for the evening meal.* He rubbed the back of his legs for just a moment and then went back to work. He did not want to be accused of being lazy. Everyone in Zagun who was old enough to work stayed busy all day, every day, picking fruit or making and selling dolls, farming or working in small shops. All to provide enough for another day. It was not easy.

But if the days were full of hard work, the nights made up for it. They were full of stories. With faces lit up by the blazing fire they sat around, the aunts spun tales about God the Storyweaver, speaking to the children of a new chapter for their families. They smiled and laughed and sang until the little ones nodded their heads in deep sleep. Ibrahim listened and watched through half-closed eyes. He was so tired, he drifted off to sleep too, listening to his aunts tell about a story more amazing than any of his dreams, a story that would never end.

In another place, at another time, a pastor with gray hair and a nice smile talked to his congregation about an amazing dream he had. In his dream, the Lord asked the church to share the resources they had been given with others far away. The pastor told the church, "This sharing isn't for us, for our people—this sharing is for someone else. But the Lord told me we will be blessed by our obedience. In fact, the sharing we do might change us more than any change we do elsewhere."

So the leaders met and talked, the church prayed and fasted, and everyone agreed. They heard the Storyweaver whispering to them about a place thousands of miles away—somewhere on the continent of Africa.

A few days passed by. On Sunday, they worshipped together. But when Monday morning came, Ibrahim noticed his mother wasn't out with the others, picking fruit. He thought he had seen her getting up a little while ago, when he was starting out to fetch water for the day. Where would she have gone?

Ibrahim was now old enough that one of his daily chores every morning and evening was to fetch the water. It was a big deal—only those who were grown up enough could take on this job. It meant walking

Fasting is what people do when they want to concentrate very hard on something they want to talk to God about. Usually it means giving up food for a certain amount of time. Read about fasting in Matthew 4:2 and Acts 14:2.

four kilometers from their hut down to the river. It took Ibrahim about forty minutes to get there and a little while longer to get back, since the jar was so heavy on his head.

When he got back, he caught one of the other aunts as she was preparing some food. "Have you seen uwata?" he asked her. "I haven't seen her all morning—but I just got back from fetching the water. Is she out working in the fields now?"

A funny look crossed her face and she shook her head.

4 kilometers = about 2.5 miles = about 44 full-size soccer fields.

"She is not well, Ibrahim." She saw the worry lines form in Ibrahim's forehead and gave him a quick pat as she bustled off to her next duty. "Just pray, child. God knows what is wrong with her. He will heal her if it's his will. Go do your work now. And keep praying."

Then Tuesday came, and his mother didn't come out of the hut at all, not even to eat. Ibrahim grew more concerned with each hour and each look that passed between the aunts. Something was badly wrong. This was not like his strong mother.

He found Daniel, one of his other "cousins." "It's been two days now, Daniel. She is sick—we must do something for her!"

Daniel was sad—Ibrahim's mother was always so cheerful and made everyone feel good. She had a big smile and was never too busy to take a moment to sit on a log or a step and listen. "But what can we do? Where can we go?" Daniel asked.

"I know the doctor who shared about Jesus with Endurance is only one village over the rocks, about two days' walking. I have heard the aunts talking about him before. I think we should try to get to him and see if he'll come treat uwata."

"How can we leave? Who will get the *ruwa* for everyone if we are missing?" Daniel asked.

Ibrahim didn't want to leave his village, but he had been praying. And he kept feeling like he must go, like he was being told to go. "They used to get it for themselves before we were big enough. Don't worry. You can stay, but I must go. She once left everything she knew for my safety. Now I must leave for hers."

POST CARD

CORRESPONDENCE

Ruwa means "water."

Not long after the church heard from the Storyweaver, they reached out to some of their African friends, men and women God had already been using to help his people find clean water. They told them of their pastor's dream and their prayers and their gathering of gifts. They talked about their shared burden for Africa, and the needs they knew their brothers and sisters had there. Could they form a partnership?

The Africans said they already knew how to drill a borehole to get clean water for a village. They knew where to look for water and which villages needed it. But they were praying for a special machine.

The Storyweaver that day brought them together for many reasons we still don't know—he had plans and purposes for those who prayed, those who gave, those who went. He had plans and purposes for those who worked, those who stayed, those who received. He is all-knowing and all-seeing, and was bringing together the story lines of many of his children.

But one of them in particular, he knew, in a year or so, was going to take a long walk . . .

Ibrahim wrapped a small amount of plantains and yams and some mangoes in a rag and placed them in his bag. He didn't want to take too much from the others, but he knew he'd need something to keep him going on this journey. He wondered if he would be able to find any water in the direction of the doctor's village. All he had to take with him was a small corked jar of water. He could not carry the heavy jugs such a long way.

With some last instructions whispered to Daniel— mainly to keep quiet about his trip until the sun was high (not wanting the aunts to try to stop him)— Ibrahim set out in the early morning darkness on his two-day walk.

Ibrahim always paid close attention when the aunts talked about other villages. He liked to think about other places and what they were like, what the people who lived there were like. He had a sharp mind and could remember everything he was told, so he felt confident that he was going the right way.

He had remembered Endurance talking about the cluster of trees where the path turned to go to the

Nearly 1 billion people in the world don't have access to clean, safe water.

rocky area. It was about midday when the trees finally came into sight. Once he reached their shade, he sat down with a *thump* and leaned against a smooth trunk. He hadn't noticed how thirsty he was until just then. He reached for his jar of water.

As he took careful sips of the cool water, he thought back to a few nights ago, when one of the storytelling aunts told them about Moses and the Israelite people. "The Israelites were whining and complaining," she had said. They were thirsty and had no water in the desert to drink. "Now Moses grew tired of those grumbling goats. And he grumbled too—to God! He was afraid of the people. But he should not have been afraid. No, no. The Storyweaver always has a plan."

Ibrahim smiled to himself. He and the children had laughed at this story when the aunt told it. God brought them water from a rock! It was so amazing, and so funny. Ibrahim had imagined the looks on the faces of those Israelites when Moses struck the dry, dead rock and out came cool, bubbling water. He took one more sip and prayed, *Thank you God, for giving us what we need.*

[Moses] called the place Massah and Meribah [meaning testing and quarreling] because the Israelites quarreled and because they tested the L ORD saying, "Is the L ORD among us or not!"
—Exodus 17:7

After eating a little, he unfolded the rag he had wrapped around his food. On the back of the rag he had marked the path that he remembered the aunts talking about. It was a rough map—he'd had only the end of a charred stick to write with at the time, but it made him feel better to have a plan. He packed his things and took one look back at the way he had come. *Please God, let me find what uwata needs.*

Later that evening, Ibrahim reached the big rocks. He found shelter under one of them, which had a kind of ledge jutting out over the ground, just high enough to allow him to wedge his body in under it. The air was still. He lay awake for a moment, listening to the screeching of the monkeys and the buzzing of insects. But these noises were the familiar soundtrack to his nights, and soon sleep overtook his mind—he was too exhausted from his journey to be concerned about wild dogs or lions.

By late afternoon on the second day, he reached the doctor's hut at last. Sheets, hung as doors, blew in the slight breeze, and he could hear moaning from inside some of the huts that were grouped together on the medical compound. *What was making all of them sick?* he wondered. *Can the doctor help all these people?* He peeked behind some of the sheets shyly, feeling awkward in this strange place. He wiped his sweaty hands on his thin pants.

He knew the doctor wouldn't know him, but maybe he would remember his mother.

"Doctor!" Ibrahim spotted the man just going into one of the huts, stethoscope around his neck. He followed him, shuffling between patients who were lying on the floor. "Doctor!"

The doctor paused and looked over to the boy, startled by his appearance. Dirty and unkempt, Ibrahim bore the marks of a young man fresh from a journey across the rocky pass.

With a few steps the doctor was by his side, taking a quick look at his eyes and mouth. "Nurse! Get this young boy some ruwa."

The doctor had him sit down on a bench while the nurse fetched the water. After

This is a doctor hut like the one Ibrahim visited.

> Lack of clean water results in more deaths than the amount that comes from any war.

several gulps, Ibrahim started to feel better. "This water is so good! I've never tasted water like this before—it tastes like fresh air! May I have more, please?" As he gained strength and courage, he spilled out his connection to Endurance, and the story of the other aunts, his cousins, and their fruit farm. He told of his mother and her sickness, and of his long journey for help.

"I have come so far—please, tell me you can help uwata," he pleaded.

The doctor asked a lot of questions, and then said, "Without seeing her, I am only guessing, but I imagine she has gotten sick from something in the river. Many people here are suffering from the same illness. I can send some medicine with you to treat her, but if she takes the pills with the dirty ruwa, she will just get sick again." The doctor rumpled up his hair in frustration.

They sat a moment in silence.

"So you mean she isn't going to get better? You can't help her?" Ibrahim asked, hoping maybe he had just misunderstood.

"Not without clean ruwa, I can't."

"Then where can we get clean ruwa? Can I carry it back? I have been able to carry water on my head for more than a year now!"

"No," the doctor said. "It's too much and too heavy for the journey. And I don't have a vehicle available to take you back right now. But we can all have clean ruwa, right where we live. It's right there in your village. God provided it under the ground for all his people."

"Your village has a river in it?" Ibrahim sounded doubtful. No one had told him of this river, and he hadn't seen it. "We don't have rivers in our village, doctor. Our water source is several kilometers away."

"Yes, son, you do. You just can't see it. It's always flowing deep under the ground."

"And that's what uwata needs? To get better?"

"Yes, that is what she needs." The doctor began preparing a small packet of medicine and a few other supplies for the boy.

Ibrahim stood straight up. "Then that's what we will pray for! You taught my aunt about Jesus, who taught uwata, who taught me. If I believe Jesus can help us with a way to the underground river, then you must believe this even more! You have known his power even longer. I bet you know even more stories than Endurance."

The doctor laughed. "You would think that is how it should work, but sometimes those who know less believe more." Words from the book of Isaiah crossed the doctor's mind: *A little child will lead them.* He placed the packet of medicine and instructions in Ibrahim's bag and handed it to him. "I will pray and send you back with something to help make your mother feel better while you are all waiting for God to answer. He will answer you, I don't know how, but never forget: you are not forgotten. He has written your name and hers in the palm of his hand."

A team of people of different colors and countries was assembled: some with gifts in giving, others with gifts in serving, some studied the Bible, some studied engineering, some studied languages. The Storyweaver worked them together, brought them into the same group, for their good as well as the good of others. He inspired and convicted and encouraged this church to help his children without clean ruwa.

Only the Storyweaver could see whose lives would be saved with clean water or whose children would now be safe because they didn't have to walk so far. He could see who would now be able to go to school, having fewer daily chores.

So the church shared and sold and gave and worked to gather the money needed for the link between the people and the underground river—the borehole machine.

Then they prayed and asked God where exactly, in all his big African garden, should they go?

From Beth's Journal

"Do you remember me?" It was a question that I think the Storyweaver had been waiting for. And the way he works, he led one person who knew another, to a conversation that led to a trip, to a machine with a purpose and an engineer with a heart to serve. He does remember, and he always has a plan.

Meanwhile, half a world away, Ibrahim found his shelter under the rock again that night. He lay there, looking at the stars. *God, do you remember me?* he prayed silently. *I came all this way to look for what uwata needs, and I'm afraid now. I'm afraid I won't be able to get it for her in time. Please, God, bring uwata what she needs.* Ibrahim fell asleep, whispering over and over again, "Ruwa, ruwa, ruwa."

"Do you remember me?" the engineer asked one of the other team members. He had spoken to them all on the phone about this project some time ago, but this was the first time they had met in person. Handshakes and smiles were exchanged, as the visiting team made its way into the village. The plan was to get started on the actual drilling today, and everyone was excited.

Two years, thousands of hours, multiple countries, lots of trips, plenty of money, and a couple of languages had brought the team to this point. They had learned lessons, resolved conflicts, trusted in God, and seen provision. Now only one thing remained—clean water coming from a well.

But before any work began, they circled together and asked, "Lord, please give us favor. We asked you where we could go, and you have brought us here. Allow us to see your story unfold here today."

Ibrahim felt like he had been walking for a week, although it was just the middle of the third day when the little cluster of trees came into sight again. He knew his village wasn't too far away, and he wanted to run and get home to his mother. But his pack was heavier now, and his tired legs would not move fast enough.

He stopped for just a few minutes under the trees to eat a little and to take a tiny sip from one of the bottles of water the doctor had sent with him. He wanted to save as much as he could for his mother to take with her medicine. This ruwa was so clean and clear and sweet. Surely it would heal her hurting body. But what would happen when there was none left?

Ibrahim packed up his bag carefully and started out on his path again. After a few more hours, familiar landmarks came into sight, and he could see the fields where his family worked.

Boom! Boom! Boom!

What was that? He had never been near a war, but he had heard stories, and it came to his mind that this is what it would sound like. But there was no fire or smoke. And there were no vehicles he could see that could make such a sound.

Boom! Boom! Boom!

Ibrahim broke into a trot, despite his tired legs. Anxiety produced a lump in his throat. He strained his ears to hear any other clues, but all he could hear was the booming rhythm, getting much louder and clearer with every step.

He was surprised to see a crowd of people gathered at the edge of the village—and not just his family. It was afternoon—why weren't they working in the fields? There were traders and people from other villages. Lots of people!

"What is this?" he shouted over the noise up to Daniel, who he'd found climbing up the side of a hut to get a better view. Daniel dropped down on the dusty ground, and the two boys embraced, their hands slapping each other's backs.

Daniel didn't answer; he just grinned a huge grin and pulled Ibrahim up with him onto the side of the hut. There was a break in the crowd, and as the people parted, Ibrahim stared with his cousin at the largest machine they had ever seen. It was so loud, he could feel the sound down deep in his stomach. The machine looked like it was digging straight into the ground. It shook the earth as it struck rock over and over again.

What are they doing? Ibrahim wondered. *And why does everyone look so happy about it?*

Not everyone. *Uwata.* Ibrahim jumped down without another word to Daniel and ran to his mother's hut as fast as he could go.

"My son." She smiled weakly at him as he entered the hut. Light streamed through where the thatched roof and the walls met, and he could see the relief on her face.

"Here, uwata, I have brought you medicine and special water from the doctor." He took one pill out of the packet, remembering the instructions the doctor  had given him. He handed the pill and the bottle of water to her gently and told her, "The doctor said these will make you feel much better." He decided not to tell her about the bad ruwa and how, once the bottles of water ran out, she would just get sick again. He didn't want to think about that.

"Son," she said, after swallowing the pill, "I was worried about you. That was too long a journey to take alone! I wish I could have talked to you before you left. I wanted to tell you—"

"Not to go, I know," Ibrahim interrupted her. "But I had to go. I felt God was telling me to go."

"No, that is not what I mean," his mother

continued, reaching for his arm. "The night before you left I had a dream. Our village, our house, was surrounded by water. Water, as far as you could see. I have been praying since then about what it means and reading in the Bible for answers, and I need you to

hear me say a few things." She pulled herself up on her elbows and leaned in, looking Ibrahim straight in the eyes. "Listen, no matter what happens, I am OK."

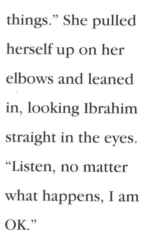

Everyone who drinks this water will be thirsty again, but whoever drinks the water I give them will never thirst. Indeed, the water I give them will become in them a spring of water welling up to eternal life.

—John 4:13, 14

Ibrahim sucked in a deep breath and squeezed her hand. She seemed to gain strength, and took another sip of water. "I may look bad now," she continued, "but I was much more sick on the inside before Endurance told me about Jesus. I was so thirsty before knowing him. I had been always looking around for something to fill me up, and when she told me about the spring of *mai pai ruwa*, I took a deep drink from it and haven't ever looked back since. I want you, Ibrahim, more than anything, to drink from that ruwa. I want you to know I left my home so that you and your sister, Esther, could come from a family that honors God. Don't ever put your trust in your own cistern, or how much ruwa you can carry on your head. Trust in the source of water that never runs dry."

She fell back on the mat, worn out from all her words and the emotion she'd poured into them. Ibrahim felt confused. He loved his mother and trusted her, and he loved Jesus too. But what was she

POST CARD

CORRESPONDENCE

Mai pai ruwa means "living water."

talking about, drinking from water that didn't run dry? And not being thirsty ever again? Mama wasn't making sense. *Maybe she is just tired*, he thought.

Days passed and the booming sound continued. Night and day the noise could be heard all over Zagun. More and more people had abandoned

their chores and daily activities to watch the machine and the people who were working it. There were more visitors, people who had walked for days from surrounding villages.

Ibrahim stayed by his mother's side most of the time, making sure she took the medicine and bringing her whatever she needed. He heard rumors about the people who had come from another country and what they were doing here, but he was too preoccupied with worry and care for his mother to take it all in.

But he felt the rhythm of the machinery and the excitement of the people building. One day Endurance stopped in at the door of his mother's hut. She was dressed in her most beautiful clothes—ones she saved for their special worship services—and she was beaming. *Wonder what's so special about today?* Ibrahim thought.

Endurance said a few words to his mother and then turned to him. "Ibrahim, some friends will come to bring your mother out. You must come with me. Come with me and hear about the ruwa, mai pai ruwa."

Ibrahim could hear singing. He was curious. *Mai pai ruwa.* There were those words again.

When they went out and joined the crowd, Ibrahim longed to be in front, to see what was happening up close. But he felt protective of his mother. So he settled for standing nearby where the men had brought her out and set her mat up on a flat rock.

God's children from afar knew they were witnessing a movement of his hand. Never mind the sacrifice it took to get here, or the time invested; as they watched the machine do its work, they believed they were a part of something eternal. They looked around at each other—a teacher, a pastor, a housewife, an engineer, and many more—all so different. All just normal people, with homes and families and work and worries of their own. They commented and laughed about how much they had grown together through the process. What those in the village experienced daily, working together with their hands for the good of everyone, they had felt themselves in a new way.

They all joined in a song together, and as they did, a man wearing a hat turned a big wheel. The cranking rhythm of the wheel seemed to be speaking, "Ruwa, ruwa, mai pai ruwa."

Spontaneously, the village began to chant, "Ruwa, ruwa, mai pai ruwa." Up front, a Nigerian pastor danced in his tribal clothes, wearing a big smile. The thumping of the machine, the singing, the chanting, the dancing—all of it seemed to blend together in one noisy and joyful chorus. The words echoed in Ibrahim's head. *Ruwa, ruwa, mai pai ruwa.* Then . . . *WHOOOSSSHHH!!!*

The music stopped. Everyone screamed, first with surprise and then in delight, as they were splashed with the water coming out of the machine. It shot way up in the sky; then the man cranked the wheel to pull it down a little, laughing and crying at the same time. People were hugging, dancing, catching water in their hands, and drinking.

No one seemed worried about the water running out. It looked like it would never stop.

Thank you, Lord, thank you, Lord, thank you, Lord, thank you, Lord. The pastor who had had the dream lifted his hands to the sky.

Ibrahim could hardly believe his eyes. He looked over at his mother. He looked at his cousin. He watched the pastor up front praying and raising his hands. He jumped off the rock he was perched on and began to run around with the other children splashing in the puddles.

"It's like a river!" shouted Esther, grabbing Ibrahim's shirt and jumping up and down. Ibrahim stopped and stared at her, then at the column of ruwa spilling onto the ground. A feeling that was like joy and relief and satisfaction mixed together ran through his body. It was like taking a drink of fresh, clean water.

This is what uwata needs, the doctor had said.

This is what uwata was talking about, a Source that doesn't run dry.

This is what I prayed for, he realized at last.

I am not forgotten.

Ibrahim looked up in the sky, raised his hands, and drank in the mai pai ruwa the Storyweaver was offering him.

More! More! I want more of you! I believe! I believe! I believe! his heart sang.

More! More of you! More of your plan! prayed the pastor who first had the dream. *More of your story!* He watched the village dance with joy over the water spilling out. *More of you! More of this!* More community, more sacrifice, more blessing. I believe! I believe! I believe!

REMEMBER THIS

Stepping out in faith is hardly ever easy. There is always some kind of sacrifice involved, and sometimes it can be very scary. But God promises that wherever we go, he will be with us. Think about where God is telling you to go. Where we go in faith, we can go in confidence.

"Therefore, brothers and sisters, since we have confidence to enter the Most Holy Place by the blood of Jesus, by a new and living way . . . let us draw near to God with a sincere heart and with the full assurance that faith brings, having our hearts sprinkled to cleanse us from a guilty conscience and having our bodies washed with pure water. Let us hold unswervingly to the hope we profess, for he who promised is faithful."
—Hebrews 10:19-23

Endurance began singing, and others soon joined in with her:

Ni zan je da yesu ko'ina

Ban damu da gargadan

hanya ba

Ni zan je, ni zan je.

I must go with Jesus

anywhere

No matter the roughness

of the road

I must go, I must go.

In this story, Ibrahim had to make a long journey all alone. Have you ever had to do something really difficult on your own? What helped you do it?

Of course, we know Ibrahim wasn't really all alone. God was with him every step of his way. Have you ever thought about going anywhere to serve God? Where would you go? How do you think it would help you to know God was with you? Write your thoughts about the story of Ibrahim here.

Chapter 4
CHRISTIANA'S MISSION

Taralincu. *Move. Have. To. Get. Out.* Divya
chanted to herself in her head. Looking around at the
room, she saw the sheet flapping over the door in the
wind. It seemed to be beckoning her to come.

Am I safe? Where is he?

She looked around the filthy room nervously.
He often stepped out for a minute at a time. He had
his routines, and she knew them all. But every now
and then he was unpredictable. Once she had peered
through a tear in the cloth covering the windows

POST CARD

CORRESPONDENCE

Divya knows Telugu, one of many Indian
languages. There are around twenty of-
ficially recognized languages in India;
however, Hindi and English are the two
official languages of the country.

Taralincu means "move."

and had watched him stand outside for most of a morning.

A noise outside now made her jump. Just a rickshaw passing by—the sounds of the morning market business were growing louder. Yet he still did not come.

Could this be my chance?

Take it! something in her screamed. *Move now!*

There were others around the room, slumped up against the walls or half buried in rags on the floor.

Others with disabilities far more severe than hers. She could not save them. The thought of leaving them all there disturbed her, but she put it out of her mind. *Just save yourself . . .*

A tiny cry came from the back of the shack. *Wait!*

There was a baby here somewhere. She had heard it crying last night and had heard the man grumbling about what he was going to do with it. It must be in the back room. *It shouldn't have to stay, shouldn't have this be its only memory.* She crept out into the dark corridor, feeling her way past each doorway, trying to guess which one to enter. *There isn't much time!* She had lived in this place for as long as she could remember, but didn't know the layout much past her own room . . .

There! It's that door.

She pushed on the rickety door, but something was blocking it from opening all the way. In the dim light she could see the bundle lying in the middle of the floor. She squeezed herself through the entrance and scooped it up. The baby wasn't crying anymore; it just looked weak—empty eyes, mouth hanging open.

Divya didn't stop to think. She just stuffed the baby inside her jacket, hurried back the way she had come, and walked right out through the sheet that had separated her from a world she had long since forgotten (and was sure had forgotten her).

It had been years—how many? Divya didn't know—since she had been outside on her own. It looked familiar in a way. She passed the street corner where he had put her to beg almost every day. But without his watchful eye, it looked like a whole other place, not quite as much of a prison as it normally seemed. She saw people walking over the spot where she usually would stand with her hand reaching out. *Why hadn't anyone ever looked at me? Or asked me if I was OK? They just dropped their change and walked away.*

Divya, feeling a bit bolder, scanned the faces in the crowd as she moved through. She wondered if her

family had ever looked for her in a crowd like this. *Do they still look for me now?* She was so small when she had been taken. The faces she could see in her mind—she didn't even know if they were faces of her family or strangers. Or if she was taken . . . or given.

It didn't really matter anymore, she supposed. Since that day, she had had nothing but long days and longer nights, standing on the corner, begging for money, avoiding him. And all for what? To make him richer, to keep his "business" going.

Enough! Don't think about that now, she chided

herself. *Taralincu. Move. Move. Escape.*

The faces all started blurring together. She was tired and thirsty, and her thoughts were jumbled. A man's loud voice made her jump again and brace herself. Her nervousness had always irritated her captor. Her jumps and twitches were usually answered with a hard slap. She squeezed her eyes shut tight now and stopped in the street, waiting for the tight grasp on her arm followed by the strike to her cheek.

But there was nothing.

She opened her eyes and looked around. Then smiled. *I am out. I got out. I escaped.*

We escaped.

She looked down at the baby she had already forgotten, tucked safely into her coat. He? She? She didn't know for sure and didn't want to stop to check now. But the baby seemed to be sleeping peacefully. Divya sighed and wondered where to go.

Will this ever get easier, Lord? Father John sat down on a bench and looked across the familiar cityscape. *I could fill the house I have and a hundred more, just with the people I see from this spot.* As the director of a home for those without anywhere else to go, Father John was out this morning, like every morning, searching the streets for those in need of his services. It was never easy, to look out over slums that stretched as far as the eye could see and know who needed his help the most. Today, though, his heart was especially heavy. He had felt God lead him that morning to fast and pray. His stomach growled, a reminder of his time in Isaiah: "They will neither hunger nor thirst, nor will the desert heat or the sun beat down on them. He who has compassion on them will guide them and lead them beside springs of water" (49:10).

I am listening, Lord. He bowed his head, his gray hair shining in the sunlight. *I want to be guided. I am looking for the water. Who will I serve today?*

A noise whistled past Divya, and she realized it was the sound of a train. All these years, from her corner, she had heard trains, but she never knew the tracks were so close. She moved forward, stumbling

The current population of India is estimated to be 1.2 billion. There are approximately 30 million orphans in India.

eventually into a station. People were everywhere, on their way to meet other people or to get to other places. No one even noticed her—a no one on the way to nowhere.

Move. Move. Escape.

She leaned against a wall, squeezed between two older men. They smelled bad, but then again, so did she. She had not bathed in a very long time. The man had always said it was better for business if she looked dirty.

She slipped past a girl collecting something. She wondered if this young woman was begging too, but she wore a uniform, and everyone was handing her pieces of paper. Divya heard the loud, rushing roar of an oncoming train and found herself pressed into the crowd and being pushed forward, almost without touching the ground. A wave of people squeezed her with the others through the opening of the train car. She wanted to cry, but no sound came out.

Where are we going?

The baby moved and Divya jumped. She wrapped her arms around her chest, instinctively protecting the baby. She peeked down at its face again. Eyes closed. It was still sleeping. Divya yawned. *She* wanted to sleep.

At the next stop, the crowd thinned out for a moment as people got off the train. Divya quickly moved to a back corner, finding a seat. She tucked her coat in more snugly around her bundle, folded her arms, and leaned her head against the wall. Sleep swallowed her up quickly.

Father John bent over his knees, resting his head in his clasped hands. *Lord, I need your glory strength. I need you to fill my cup. My hope is in you. My heart is so heavy with the needs I see all around. Just last night, we had to turn away some more widows. Was that a right decision? Did you want us to trust more for your provision? It's too hard to discern sometimes. Will you bring me the children and adults you specifically want us to minister to? There are children and babies, widows and disabled. There are the unemployed and the unemployable. There are addicts and the sick. Lord, I know you see each one. I just don't know where to start today.*

The whistle from a local train caused him to look up for a moment. From his perch up on this hill he could see crowds starting to flow through the markets, and he could hear the buzzing of a city going about its day.

So many people. So many stories. He continued praying, *This is your story, today and every day. Write me in it wherever and however you will . . .*

Divya woke up a few times over the next two days, usually when the train rolled to a stop at a busy station. She didn't even attempt to get off—no one would be there to greet her. The train ride got longer and the pangs of hunger grew sharper, but she saw no food on board. After a while, her hunger died. She didn't have any idea where she was or where she was headed. She struggled to focus, but she was so very sleepy.

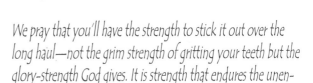

We pray that you'll have the strength to stick it out over the long haul—not the grim strength of gritting your teeth but the glory-strength God gives. It is strength that endures the unendurable and spills over into joy.

—Colossians 1:11, 12 (*The Message*)

Sometimes she would wake up and feel the wetness of the baby on her. But that hadn't happened since when—maybe yesterday afternoon? The hours seemed all blurred together. Divya felt up under her coat and in the folds of the blanket wrapped around the baby. Dry. It had been dry now all day.

"Who is this? Does she have any ID?" She heard voices over her head. Lights were flashing in her eyes.

She jumped and clutched her chest. Hands were touching her and grasping her arms. She recoiled and braced herself.

Taralincu. Move. Move. Escape.

But she couldn't move. She had no strength. In her tired mind she tried to fight, but in reality, she was easily carried off the train.

Father John reached for his phone when he felt it buzzing. The railway protection force was calling; they had found a young, mute, possibly mentally disabled woman with an infant. "If someone was with them, they are long gone now. We have no ID and she hasn't made a sound. It'll be touch and go with the baby—she's pretty dehydrated—but it's right up your alley. Are you interested? Will you come and claim them?"

Father John looked up and whispered, "Where you lead, I will follow. Show me how to help these two with the love of a father." Then he spoke into the phone, "Yes, I will be right there."

Divya woke up with a start. There were strange noises, lights, faces. She was dressed in a clean *sari*. *Where are my clothes?* She was so hungry. Reaching for her stomach, she realized the baby was gone. *Oh no! Where did it go?* She tried to get the attention of a person walking by, but no one understood her.

No one ever understands me.

Falling back on her mat, she was filled with despair. It was the same problem as always. Even when she tried to speak, no one ever heard her.

A nurse motioned to a man down the hall. "Father, I think she is awake." A man in a dark suit hurried into the room and leaned over Divya's bed. Forgetting for a moment that she couldn't talk, he

POST CARD

PON NCE

A mute person is someone who cannot speak, either as a result of brain or other physical damage, or sometimes as a result of abuse or a mental disorder that results in extreme anxiety.

Mute means "unable to speak."

asked, "Can you hear me, dear? What is your name? Do you know where you are?" His voice sounded kind, compassionate.

Divya motioned to her stomach, waving frantically. Father John understood. "The baby you had with you is safe. She was dehydrated and is still very weak. We are taking good care of her and praying for her to recover. Is she your baby?"

She wanted to tell him her story—how she had lived with a stranger for years, how he'd hurt her and others like her, others who couldn't tell. *No, the baby isn't mine*, she thought, *but it's the closest thing to mine I've ever had*. Sighing deeply, she leaned back. She feared they would take the baby away from her. But this place felt different. Safe. It smelled nice. *I am not shaking. Maybe I can make him understand.* Her thoughts jumbled again and she tried to focus. Father John talked quietly to her for a few moments, reading from a book on his lap. She drifted back to sleep.

Father John closed his Bible and fingered the old, well-worn leather cover. He studied the young woman in the bed closely, looking for any clues to who she might be. Her appearance when she was brought in seemed to be that of a beggar, but it was hard to say. The nurses had said her hair was so matted they had to wash it five times before they could get a comb through it. They had also told him of many bruises they found on her arms and back. Who was she? Where had she come from?

Her breathing became more regular. It was certain he was not going to get any answers from her just now, and she probably needed time. He made a note to himself to remind the nurses to get her some paper to write on. There was a good chance she could not read or write, but perhaps she could draw some answers for them.

In the days that followed, Father John traveled between the homes he managed, checking on the children in the orphanage, buying the rice for next week's dinner outreach for widows, visiting the halfway house for the men who were transitioning out of prison. He continued his fast for the health of the infant girl, and prepared a bed for the woman in the small shelter they had for disabled adults.

How many days have passed now? Divya didn't know; she just kept sleeping and waking up. Each time

A young woman wearing a sari, a typical Indian woman's garment.

she awoke, it took a few minutes to remember she wasn't back in her old room. She ate a few bites of whatever they offered her, scooping it up with her hands, but she wasn't used to eating a lot at one time. Sometimes Father John was there when she woke up, though it took her a few minutes to remember him too.

He had brought in the baby that morning for her to see. She could tell by the baby's clothes that it was a girl. The baby cried, and everyone smiled. She could tell the cries meant something good. She, too, liked hearing the noise. Father John had asked her once before if the baby had a name, and Divya had told him no, shaking her head. Now he was saying something about names, and asking if he could name the baby Christiana.

Christiana. I like it, she thought. Smiling, she nodded yes. She heard him say something about a Christian name and "her destiny reborn." *I wonder what he means?*

It is time to move the girls to the home full-time, Father John thought. There they would join dozens more caught in difficult chapters of their stories. He pictured faces of many he had known—some stayed for a while; others, their whole lives. But whoever was there at night around the dinner table, he thanked God for each one of them.

He told his staff later that morning, "The baby is getting stronger every day; let's make sure she gets a chance to see her mother often. I am still not convinced the woman can manage her care alone, but let's keep them connected. I'm told that inside one of the mother's shirts was written the name Divya. I've used that name with her, and I can tell she responds to it and understands me, even though it seems she cannot speak. Let's all keep talking to her, whenever we can, and share stories with her from the Bible. She is easily frightened, but that seems to calm her more than anything else."

Divya turned quickly at the sound of footsteps. She had been sitting up in her bed and looking at pictures in a book one of the nurses had given her. Another nurse walked in with some new clothes.

"Hello, Divya, how are you this afternoon?"

Divya smiled her response.

"That's good, Divya." The nurse waited a moment, then said gently, "Divya, you are doing so well, you are going to leave here today."

Divya's heart started racing. *Leave? Where will I go?*

The nurse couldn't hear her question, but she could read Divya's big eyes. "You are going home with Father John and some of his friends." Then she leaned down and whispered, "Not everyone is so lucky. Be glad that you have a place to go." She helped Divya into her new clothes and packed up the few little things she had collected during her days there.

"I know the plans I have for you," declares the LORD, "plans to prosper you and not to harm you, plans to give you hope and a future.

—Jeremiah 29:11

Divya didn't know where she was going, but if Father John was there, she decided it could only be good. The kind man had visited her every single day since she had come to the clinic and had said more words to her than she ever remembered anyone ever saying to her in the past. Divya ran her hand over the cover of the colorful book she was holding to her chest. He read stories to her—good stories about a Storyweaver who loves her and hasn't forgotten her. She didn't understand them all, but she liked the sound of Father John's voice. Wherever he wanted to take her and the baby sounded OK to her.

In the years that followed, Father John met hundreds of people. But he always remembered the girls God used to answer his prayer that morning he looked out over the city, wondering who needed his help the most. Since that day, whenever he began to feel overwhelmed by the needs around him, he would fast and ask God to make the next move. Every time he saw Divya or Christiana, he remembered that shift in his listening—the time he started listening to what God wanted to tell him, instead of just looking for the answers he wanted to hear.

He felt committed to the growth of both the child and her mother, and was updated regularly on Christiana's excellent progress. At age ten, she was leading her class.

Father John thought of many young women he had known over the years—women with sharp minds and amazing skills. He wondered where they all were now. He knew the stories of some of them. They had gone out into the world and found it impossible to fight against a culture that denied their rights, their need for education, and their value. He didn't want that for Christiana.

He had been talking to a director of a nearby school—they were interested in Christiana coming to continue her education there. *Lord,* he prayed, *show me how to come alongside what you have designed for this girl—the next chapter of her life.* He knew it would be hard to separate her from Divya, but he wanted to give her a chance to grow.

"Amma," Christiana said, addressing Divya as her mother. "Show me again—how fast did I grow that year?" Divya answered in her usual way, by putting her hands almost together and then quickly spreading them far apart. Her eyes sparkled as Christiana laughed. It was a story they had relived together many times—neither one ever tired of it. Christiana only knew what little she could get Divya to show her in pictures or through motions—but it was enough to make a very good adventure story. How on that day God had given Divya courage she had never had, and had pushed her onto that train, and brought her all the way to Father John's care. There were many gaps in the story. But Christiana

Only 30 to 40 percent of Indian girls are educated in schools.

had decided that though Divya couldn't answer all her questions, there was One who had all the answers, and she would be content with that.

As Christiana grew and her reading improved, she told Divya the same stories Father John had begun reading to her years before—stories of a God who moved his children in and out of each other's lives, like trains on the tracks that wove across the country, for purposes they may never even fully realize.

That day, after Christiana had left, Divya busied herself with the small tasks she was asked to do around the home. As she smoothed out the fresh linens, she thought about what God had done for her and for Christiana. How he had taken a tangled mess of despair and abuse and darkness and smoothed it out into a path leading to hope and health and light. And all she had had to do was have the courage to listen to his voice. He had said, "Move." And she had moved.

As she wrapped up some dirty clothes to go to the laundry, she thought of how much Christiana had grown, from a forgotten little bundle in a back room to the beautiful, loving child she was now. *You did not forget her, Lord.* Divya caught sight of herself in the bathroom mirror. *And you did not forget me.*

One hot day in July, when Christiana was nearly fourteen, she came after classes were over to visit Divya, as she usually did. Only this time, Divya noticed her nurse standing nearby, watching her oddly, almost like she was waiting for some show to begin. Christiana was smiling, but her eyes looked sad. "I am too old now to live here in the house with you and the others. Father John says I am *curukaina*, and that I need to study." Biting her lip, she looked away from Divya's piercing eyes.

Divya's heart swelled. *Smart?* She had always known Christiana was smart, from the time she was a little baby. She was always looking around, with big eyes taking in everything she saw. Divya was so proud. She started to hug her, but Christiana rushed ahead, "He knows of a house—the people there say I can live with other kids, other kids like me." She stumbled over her words, "Kids . . . who, who don't have a home, or people—parents—who can care for them." Divya's hands dropped to her lap. She knew she was not Christiana's mother—and could never take care of her like parents should—but she still liked to think of the girl as her own.

Divya started to turn away, but Christiana continued, "Remember those people? Those people who

POST CARD

CORRESPONDENCE

Curukaina means "smart."

came last year at Christmas and sang for us?" Divya nodded. She could picture the flowers the people had brought to hang around their necks. Christiana reached out for Divya's hand. "I don't want to leave you, but I need to study. I *want* to study. And those people can help me. I feel this pounding in my heart to get out, to escape. To make a way, for *us*. And this is the only way."

Escape. Divya sighed. It's a feeling she remembered well. But it would be so hard not to see the girl every day. She squeezed Christiana's hand and looked into her eyes. *Does that squeeze say everything I want it to?* She motioned her to go, hoping she wouldn't misunderstand her. *I don't want her to see me cry.*

Christiana gave her a hug, and hot tears burned in her eyes. She understood. She always understood.

Divya watched them drive away. *She was never mine, God, but it still feels like I am losing something.*

Father John helped Christiana in the process of moving from the adult home to the orphanage, a children's home called RestNest. It was hard to separate the two women, whose relationship he had stopped trying to figure out long ago. Families sometimes adopt children and children sometimes adopt families. He wasn't ever sure what was the case here, but no one seemed caught up in the fine print. Watching them together was for him confirmation of the truth of the words of one of his favorite psalms: "God sets the lonely in families" (Psalm 68:6).

After Christiana had moved and settled into the room she would share with the other girls, Father John brought her a gift of a few books and some notebooks. As he was leaving, he noticed the sadness in her face. He sat back down beside her. "You remember, even Jesus needed to leave his family to go study once, yes? Can you imagine what a day that was for him? Leaving the safety of those he knew and stepping into the middle of all those well-educated, intimidating older men? But he had questions to ask and things to learn. And so do you." He smiled at her and got up to leave again. "Jesus' family did not forget him. And the same is true for you. You will not be forgotten."

Christiana's eyes landed on one of the home's signs: RestNest. She sighed. So far this place had not been one of rest. She was having to learn everything all at once—the kids, the workers, the system, the way to school. This morning she had gotten turned around again and had to be led to her class by one of the older girls. She felt so embarrassed and frustrated. *How am I ever going to know it all?*

The walls were a shade of gray that matched her mood, and the lighting was bad for reading. At night she tried to sleep, her mat providing a thin layer between her and the dirt floor. But it was difficult, especially in those first few weeks. She could hear the other girls crying, and she guessed they were missing their mothers, or whoever they had known as family. She allowed her own mind to drift to Divya. But instead of tears, this brought smiles. Christiana liked thinking about where Divya was, knowing she was safe, and that she was probably thinking of her tonight too. *She will not forget me.*

As the nights and days passed, Christiana began to feel more comfortable about the children's home. And as was expected, she excelled in school. Her teachers were always complimenting her on the thoroughness of her homework. Christiana liked school, and she loved pleasing her teachers.

One day during a free time, a girl sat down beside her as Christiana watched the others chasing after a soccer ball. "How come you don't ever run around with us?" the girl asked bluntly.

"I can't do it very well, or for very long." Christiana repeated the answer she'd been given all her life. "My heart is weak—something happened to me when I was a baby, and it just doesn't work as well as it should." The other girl twisted one of her braids awkwardly, and Christiana could sense she was uncomfortable. She hurried to add, "But it's OK. I really like to watch all of you. And sometimes I just like to read. Father John tells me I'm exercising a different kind of muscle."

The girl smiled at the mention of the man's name. Everyone liked Father John. "Yes, I've seen you—you have your nose in a book all the time." She giggled, and Christiana realized she was just teasing her. It felt good to think maybe she could make some friends here. "Well," the girl added, "if you ever want to draw chalk pictures or do something else, just come get me. I like to play sports, but not all the time. And maybe some of your smarts will rub off on me!"

The girl ran off to join the group and Christiana waved to her. *Maybe I won't be so lonely here.* Besides, she had made herself a promise. When she

There are 40 to 80 million people with disabilities living in India. Children with disabilities are five times more likely not to receive an education.

had been there only a few days, she had decided that no matter what, she was going to be grateful for this opportunity to learn and study as much as she could. She knew there were lots of girls like her, like Divya, who never even had the chance to go to school for one day.

Sometimes, whenever one of the workers was going to the other home for a meeting or to help out, Christiana could get a ride to visit Divya. As the years passed, Christiana realized more and more how limited Divya's understanding was of their situation. But that didn't bother her—she liked to see her and tell her all about her classes.

Christiana stood in the doorway, waiting for

Divya to notice her. "It's me, Christiana." She always spoke softly—knowing how Divya would still jump at loud noises. Divya's face lit up at the sound of her voice. Her eyesight was weakening as she grew older, but Divya always knew Christiana's voice—even the sound of her footsteps were familiar to her. Divya didn't make any sound for anyone except for Christiana. She tried to communicate to the girl how glad she was to see her.

My girl! My daughter—so beautiful you are! She touched Christiana's cheek. The girl had long since grown accustomed to Divya's strained noises and gestures. She wrapped her arms around the only mother she had ever known.

They would spend the next hour or whatever

time they had together—Christiana telling stories about her education, about her dreams for the future. "I think about becoming a doctor or a teacher or even a lawyer. What do you think? I don't know what I want to do exactly yet. I just want to help people. Father John says I can do anything through Christ—he gives glory strength. I believe him."

Divya just kept nodding and smiling at her. She didn't know what Christiana meant, but she loved the sound of her voice.

Father John struggled up the flight of stairs to the second floor of the clinic and remembered his doctor's warnings: "I don't know how much longer you have— your heart is weakening each year. You need to rest more now than ever."

Rest! Humph! I would rather go out with a bang, he reasoned to himself. *I am ready to come home to you, Lord, but what about the homes here? Who will take over? They are growing larger every year. The problems of the world only seem to multiply. Someone must protect these people who are so vulnerable. Someone must listen to their stories. Who will come to take my place?*

Silence.

Great, more waiting. Leaning against the banister, he lifted himself up another step. *Better call someone quick, Lord. I don't know how much longer I can do this.* He made it to the top of the steps and walked through a door to see yet another new patient in the clinic. He took his Bible from under his arm. Down the hall the nurses could hear his friendly voice boom, "Good morning! I'm Father John. Why don't we start this morning with the story of Daniel?"

The nurses from Divya's home brought her to Christiana's university to celebrate with her the special day—graduation day. As they were talking over lunch, one of the nurses asked her what her final grades were.

"I did well," Christiana replied. "They said I could work anywhere I wanted." She looked at Divya, and her voice broke as she tried to explain. "There are not many of us— Indian col-lege ed-u-ca-ted wom-en." She said it slowly, emphasizing every syllable so Divya could understand better. "They told me my education is my ticket to important places.

That I can do big things . . . for others."

This time it was she who had trouble making a sound. She struggled with how to express all she wanted to say to Divya. *How do I tell her thank you?*

"I don't know where I will go yet. There are many offers. But I do know that I want women all over this country to know their worth, for people to know the value daughters bring to their home. You did that for me." *Without ever saying a word.* "I wish you could tell me which offer to accept." Christiana sighed. "Some mean more study, some mean moving away for a while. Mostly I just want to spend my life doing for others what you and Father John and the nurses from the home did for me . . . so wherever I can do that, that is where I will go . . ." Her voice trailed off.

Divya looked away. *She's leaving again. That's what she is saying. Oh Lord, when she is gone, who will hear me? And who will watch over her? Where will you lead her?*

Father John, chai tea in hand, was alone on the bench he frequented during his morning rounds. *How many times have you met me here, Lord? A thousand would be too few.* He took a few sips of his tea. *Tell me, who shall take this responsibility from me? Can you just tell me? Who will see the people with your eyes, and understand them as more than a program, or a mouth to feed? Who has that kind of understanding—to see a soul to touch, a heart to win, a person to know?* He looked down at his sandals. "Beautiful are the feet of those who bring good news!" he quoted aloud (Romans 10:15). *Whose feet are you preparing?*

In the quietness of his mind, long trained to hear the whispers of the Savior he served, he heard the name.

A Christian name. A destiny reborn.

Christiana.

Tears filled his eyes. *Thank you, Lord, thank you.*

Hundreds of miles from Divya and Father John, Christiana was busy moving into her new flat, her sari flapping as she took quick strides back and forth, carrying boxes. She couldn't wait to get started in her new job, working with a state-level government program, recruiting girls to return to school. She couldn't believe this opportunity; the salary was more than she had ever imagined earning. She hoped it would be enough for her to one day bring Divya to live here with her.

She was scared to be alone; she didn't know anyone in her new city. But she jumped at the chance to move when she heard how much responsibility she was going to have. She was so grateful for the doors her education had opened. So grateful for all the people who had made it possible.

She was putting some books on her new shelves when the phone rang.

"I am so sorry, Christiana." The voice on the other end sounded sad. "I have news about Father John. It was his heart . . . he's gone home to be with Jesus." Even through her sobs, Christiana could recognize the voice of one of the nurses from the home where Divya still lived. Christiana asked her a few questions and then hung up.

She curled up on her mat on the floor—just like she used to do as a child—and let the tears come. She thought of the thousands of hours and hundreds of conversations she had shared with Father John. *Lord, you know how important he was to me, how much he believed in me and sheltered me. You sent me to him, trusting him with my mother and my studies. He taught me about you! Why does he have to be gone now? I still have so much to learn, more to ask him! Why now?*

She paced numbly around her apartment the rest of the afternoon, finishing up the details of her move and planning for the travel she would embark on the next day. She longed to see Divya.

Early the next morning, Christiana boarded the train and found a seat in the back. She had brought along some things to read, hoping to make the long journey pass more quickly. But the flood of emotions combined with the exhaustion of moving had taken its toll. Within an hour, she was sound asleep.

Hours later she woke with a start. Something was poking her in the side. Groggily, she looked down and saw a bundle on the seat next to her. A little foot had escaped the tightly wound blanket and was kicking out with force and frustration.

Railways are the primary mode of transportation in India. The country has the most extensive rail network in the world.

"Hey, hey, little guy, don't fret." She picked up the baby and looked around, wondering where the mother was. She noticed the care with which the baby had been swaddled in the blanket and thought, *Someone was just here. This blanket is fresh.*

Christiana began to ask around of the other passengers, "Where is the mother? Anyone see the mother?" No one looked her in the eye, and no one had any answers. The baby started to cry, and she jiggled it up and down, patting its back. "Shh, shh . . . it's OK. We'll find her. Don't worry. You'll be OK."

The train stopped at the next station, and peo-ple entered and exited. Christiana scanned the crowd, looking for any clue, anyone who might belong to this baby. But no one came to claim it. At a stop an hour later, a woman on her way out leaned down and whispered in Christiana's ear, "I think the mother exited the train a couple of hours ago. I saw her crying and then shuffle out." She looked down at the baby, now sleeping peacefully. "Don't worry—I think he likes you."

Likes me? What does that even mean? Hours

later, when Christiana's stop came, she stepped off the train, determined to take the baby and report him to the authorities, then deliver him to the very home that was her destination. She thought about how she had come to pay respects to Father John. *Somehow it is fitting that I'd find a baby on this trip.* She pulled the blanket over the baby's head a little, shifted the weight of her bags on her shoulders, and started walking down the platform.

"Christiana! Welcome!" The nurses all shouted when they saw her, happily bringing Divya into the room so the reunion would be complete.

"Who is this you have with you?" One nurse set to work relieving Christiana of her baggage and took the blanket-wrapped bundle from her arms. All eyes were on Christiana as the nurse unwound the blanket and revealed the little face tucked inside.

"I found him on the train. I don't know what

happened. Someone left him right next to me. I didn't know what to do, so I asked everyone. But I think his mother abandoned him." She sighed heavily, feeling exhausted and a little annoyed. "So I brought him here." Everyone gathered around to admire the baby, who miraculously kept sleeping through all the attention.

"Hmm . . . correction. You brought *her* here." The nurse finished removing the soiled clothing and pointed to the now naked baby girl, smiling up at the huddle around her.

"Ohh," Christiana softly gasped. "They must have been hiding her in boy's clothes to trick someone who didn't want her. It's so cruel what some will

From Beth's Journal

"I am a promise, I am a possibility." As a kid I used to sing this song at the top of my lungs around my house. And I learned this truth—that inside all of us is a promise. It's a promise that we have great value. Down the road, it was tempting to let others dim the light God had turned on inside me. But each time I saw myself fade, I would think about this song, and remember who God made me to be.

do with baby girls.
I was thinking
such awful
thoughts about
that mother
all afternoon,

There has been a significant decline in the number of girls born in India over the last decade. Also, some studies suggest that, over the last decade, 35 million women in India have "disappeared."

but maybe she was trying to save her." The nurses looked at her curiously; they were well aware of what some would do and what Christiana had seen in her young life. It was their job every day to pick up the pieces in lives just like this one—a responsibility they saw less like a job and more like a calling.

"Well, can she stay?" Christiana pleaded softly. "I will call the authorities and see if anyone has reported missing a baby. But if we can't find her family, I can't think of a better place for her to grow up. And I know a little of what I am talking about." Her eyes sparkled as she looked around at the women who had served her for so many years. She began to feel a bit hopeful for the first time that day.

"Normally, we would ask Father John what to do, but under the circumstances . . ." The head nurse's voice broke. "We don't know who to ask. We don't know what will happen to the homes or all the children, or all of us." The women all looked at one another and then at Christiana. Some wiped away a few tears, and others turned away to hide their grief, still so fresh.

Christiana hugged them all tightly. "Listen, you taught me, remember? There are always more questions in life than answers, but what do we know for sure? The Storyweaver is writing a chapter for this place right now as we speak. You know it's true. There are no surprises to him. In fact, he has been moving in advance for this day. He knew it would come. We can trust that. Father John would tell us to sit down in the front row and watch the story unfold."

She choked back her own tears. And then she composed herself, as a wave of confirmation passed through her mind. "Until we know who it is the Lord

is calling to walk in Father John's steps, I will roll up my sleeves and help you myself. I don't start work for another month, and I can learn my way around that city later."

She looked down and smiled at the baby she had been irritated with just hours ago. "I'll begin my work with you, little one. What should we call you?" The little girl was now lying contentedly in her arms, eyes open. Christiana looked around the room. No one had a suggestion.

"How about Taarini? 'One who saves others.'

Someone I once loved taught me how powerful it is to rename your destiny." She smiled down at Taarini and rocked her in her arms.

Christiana finished up some details in her office and then made the rounds in the home, stopping to sit with Divya for a minute and check in on Taarini. As was her routine, she prayed with every step she made down the hallways. *Lord, thank you for this year, and for last year. Thank you for the next one and the rest. I don't know where I am headed anymore than I know where I am from, but I trust you. I know I am not forgotten. Lead me, so I can lead others.*

Christiana had assumed the responsibilities of the work Father John had started, and under her direction the ministry had grown. There had been opposition at first—there was always opposition—but she had been facing that her whole life. Some felt maybe she couldn't handle the responsibilities as a young, single woman. But she had set to work with all her heart and mind and felt content fulfilling her daily duties. Those who first doubted her were now her biggest advocates.

Dear Christiana,
The Lord whispered to me your next mission. I must say I am not surprised. He has gifted you . . .

She regularly asked God for his peace to continue, and reread a hundred times the note she had found addressed to her, waiting in Father John's desk: "Dear Christiana, The Lord whispered to me . . ."

One year became five, and five years more marked ten. It was a busy life, but no matter how busy she got, she still made a point of seeing Divya and Taarini every day. She whispered to Divya her continued gratefulness for their relationship and shared stories she lived throughout the weeks, battling government officials and walking through the slums most mornings, talking to donors and visiting jails. She bounced off the insights she was gaining from the Bible, and even though Divya never commented back, it was good to have someone who just listened to her, without expectations.

With Taarini, she shared *kulfi* and study dates, encouraging her to be all God created her to be, to have her eyes open for the destiny he was unfolding for her. Taarini looked up to Christiana and couldn't wait for her visits. It was during those visits Christiana would remember why she was working so hard, and would laugh away any tension from the day during a fun jump-roping or hopscotching session.

It was on Taarini's way to school one day, while

POST CARD

Kulfi is the Indian version of ice cream. It contains spices such as cardamom, saffron and cinnamon.

she was thinking about some things Christiana had read to her from the Bible, that she noticed a young girl asleep on the street corner, with her leg stretched out into the street itself. She thought she had seen the girl there before, and walked over to get a closer look. *How old could she be? Doesn't she know she could get run over here?* She didn't look like more than three or four years old. When Taarini went closer, she noticed some coins on the ground by the little girl's side. Not sure what to do, Taarini decided to wait and ask Christiana if she knew what this was all about. She gently pushed the girl's leg back so it wasn't hanging so far out into the street. She left a corner of *chapati* tucked under the red sleeve of the girl's smock and said a little prayer for her, asking God to bring her the bread of life that Christiana had told her about in their last conversation.

"Auntie," Taarini began the next day's discussion. "Why would a little girl be sleeping on a street corner? And why would she have coins just lying on the ground beside her?" She took a bite of her curried rice, scooping it up with her right hand.

Christiana sighed in response. "I didn't know they had returned to the area, but that probably means the gypsies are back. They

The Indian unit of money is the rupee. Right now, $1 is worth about 50 rupees. It costs about $15 to educate a child for a year in India.

are travelers, people who move from place to place, mainly begging to make money to keep themselves going. They take orphaned children they find in the street and keep them up all night, then place them somewhere around the city where they will sleep all day. People feel sorry for the children, and toss a coin or two at them as they pass by." She noticed the worried frown on the ten-year-old's face. "Tell me which corner you saw her on, and I will visit there tomorrow."

The next day, Christiana went to the spot Taarini told her about, but the child was gone. Taarini checked the same corner every day for the next month, but didn't see the girl again. "Don't worry," Christiana had told her. "When the time is right, God will make a way for your stories to cross again. If he caused her to stand out to you, then it's for a reason. In the meantime, don't underestimate how God can use your prayers for her."

Weeks passed, then a month more. Taarini prayed each night for the girl on the corner. She wondered where she was now, who was caring for her. She prayed for her health, her safety, her questions. She prayed for her belly to be full and her mat soft.

Taarini loved the RestNest home, where she lived. Even with its limited resources, it was a warm and

POST CARD

CORRESPONDENCE

Chapati is a kind of Indian bread.

loving place. She wanted every child to feel the security she had felt there. She knew her own story—how she had been left on a train and had kicked Christiana awake. Christiana always told her that her little foot was just the beginning of a big wake-up call for her that day. Christiana treated her like family, but Taarini knew she was different from most kids, like the kids at her school—kids who had parents.

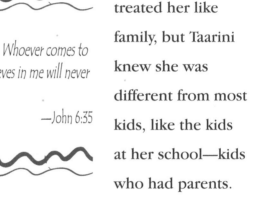

Then Jesus declared, "I am the bread of life. Whoever comes to me will never go hungry, and whoever believes in me will never be thirsty."

—John 6:35

Some days when she felt down, she wondered why her parents had left her all alone. At those times she remembered Christiana's words: "Don't focus on the fact that you were left behind. Focus on the fact that you were left to be saved. And you were left for me. You were not forgotten."

Taarini was confident in the fact that she was

surrounded by people now who loved her. She had
Christiana, and she had the nurses. And she was
learning about the Father God and his love for her.
And most nights, even the very lonely ones, that was
enough.

Who does that girl on the corner have, Father?
Who will remember her?

It was a Friday, and while Taarini was on her
way home from school, walking in a pack of other

children, she noticed a police car in front of her orphanage. She began to run toward the entrance, pushing aside the people who had gathered in the street to watch. A million questions flooded through her mind, *"Is someone hurt? in trouble? Are they going to close us down? take us away? Did someone steal from us again?"*

As she reached the gate, she noticed in the backseat of the police car were a half-dozen children, all dressed in rags, and clearly unbathed. They were shuffled from the car to the front door, and Christiana was there ushering them into the dining hall.

Taarini rushed over to Christiana, "What are you doing here? It's still the middle of the day, and you don't usually come until dinnertime. Who are these children? Why are the police here?" Her face was flushed; her large eyes showed concern and fear.

Christiana smiled at Taarini and bent down to look at her. "Oh, Taarini," she said softly, "'one who saves,' after you told me about the gypsy girl, I inquired at the police station and told them if they ever rounded up the orphaned children, I would take them in. I didn't know where we would put them, and I still don't know how we will feed them, but I knew we needed to do something. I didn't hear anything for more than a month, but this afternoon I received a call. They had found six of them. I am sure there are more, but this is a start, and they should start talking soon about where the rest might be." She straightened herself up and squeezed Taarini's hand. "We need to earn their trust first. Maybe you can help with that. Did you see them all yet? Is one of them the girl you've been praying for?"

Taarini hardly heard her question;

she was already pushing her way through the doors to see for herself. With her heartbeat pounding in her ears, she scanned the room, looking for the face that had broken into her dreams and filled her prayer times. Her heart sank. *She isn't here.*

Taarini turned back to join the other students filing in from school, now lining up as they did every day to get their chapati for lunch.

There. A flutter of red caught her eye.

It was the red sleeve she had tucked her chapati under so many weeks ago! Taarini ducked her head under the table next to her. Hiding beneath it, a little girl had curled herself up into a ball and looked as if she was going to cry. *That's her!* The girl she had seen sleeping many weeks ago now looked very much awake, and scared.

Taarini squatted down and then slowly crawled over to the girl, singing quietly as she went. It was a new song they had only recently learned in chapel. *Even if she doesn't understand what it means,* Taarini thought, *she might like the sound.*

The girl peeked at Taarini through the fingers she was hiding behind. She moved away an inch. Taarini smiled and moved forward an inch. Then she slid a bracelet off her ankle—an old, woven yarn bracelet that she had from one day when Christiana had made decorations and jewelry with her. Though it was worn, the colors were still bright. Christiana had told her the gold stood for the golden crown of the King of kings, and the green was to remind us he is the giver of all good gifts—even the green plants that bring us food to eat. The blue stood for the living water he offered everyone to drink, and the red was for the blood he shed for the sins of all, a sacrifice he made to save everyone.

The four colors were woven together. "To

remind us that the Storyweaver has designed a plan for us all—a plan that includes us weaving in and out of each other's lives," Christiana had said, "like trains on tracks. Or like little baby feet that kick their fellow passengers." Taarini smiled wider at the memory and held the pretty bracelet out to the little girl, offering it to her silently.

It's OK, I am not in any hurry, she tried to say with her eyes. *I have been praying for you every night for weeks, and I know the Storyweaver has heard me. He brought you here because he has a plan for you, and one for me, and they might even be woven together! Are you afraid? Don't be! You'll get used to this place. It might be unfamiliar, and there might be somebody you miss, but we seem to get what we need here right on time. The Storyweaver sends to us his gifts through his children. Have you ever opened one of his gifts? No? I have a feeling he is sending you one right now. He sure knows about you and has moved a lot of hands to protect you. It must be something big, your story line. Look at all the people he's already involved. I am going to take a seat in the front row and watch it unfold. I have a feeling it's gonna be good.*

You are not forgotten.

REMEMBER THIS

"Who will I serve?" Do you ask yourself this question? Do you think you'll get an answer today, or do you think that answer is somewhere far off in your future? You do not have to wait until someone hands you a secret mission envelope or until you are hired for a job. You can start serving today, right where you are. The people you serve may be ones you know—your brother or sister, your mom or dad, or your teacher or pastor—or they may be strangers. Be on the alert! Whether you are rich or poor, tall or short, older or younger—God has work he has created just for you to do. He may put opportunities right in your path, or you may have to look more closely or walk a bit out of your way to find his clues. Just don't forget to keep looking for the mission he has for you.

In this chapter, we could really see how the Storyweaver wove the lives of different people together to help others. Have you ever seen this happen in your life? Who are some people you know or have heard about who are good examples of servants of God? What parts of yourself do you think you need to work on in order to be a good servant? Write your thoughts about the story of Christiana here.

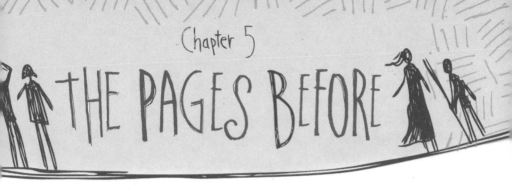

Chapter 5
THE PAGES BEFORE

It would be easy to read these chapters, put down this book, and forget about it. But the Storyweaver began writing these stories long before the days recorded in these pages, and he is writing still.

In the first chapter, you read about a man named Edgar, who wanted to teach the children he served about trusting God. They had no money and no food. A four-year-old orphan, Joel, asked him a simple question. Edgar led him to lean on his faith for the answer.

Edgar's mother was also an orphan. Her mother died, and her father, needing to work and overwhelmed with grief, left her to be cared for permanently with some extended family. One Sunday morning when she was twelve, she heard a sermon about "asking God for whatever you need in his name," and that night in bed, she prayed, begging God for the chance to meet her father, just once.

All she wanted was to see his face.

While she was praying, she heard voices in the kitchen. Moments later, the man she called "uncle" called her to come out of her room.

There, standing in the kitchen, was her father.

He was a truck driver and had been on his way through the town. He had decided to stop by to see how his daughter had grown. They sat that night and visited, and although her living situation didn't change, her faith sure did.

When she eventually married and had her own family, including a son named Edgar, she told that story "a thousand times." She taught her children to have faith in a God who always hears our prayers.

Edgar has taught that lesson to the hundreds of children God has placed in his home over the years, just like Joel. Each of those children will grow up and go on with their lives. Who knows where they will one day take those lessons? The storyweaving continues . . .

Sometimes our teachers are those who are older than us. And sometimes lessons come from unexpected places. In chapter 2, you met Seraphina, a dump diver, as they are called—someone who has so little, what others throw away becomes a treasure to her. She had nothing of material value to offer anyone, but she gave Brian a lesson in generosity that was priceless. Brian learned that whatever you give, no matter whether it is a billion dollars or a bologna sandwich, God multiplies it. It's the craziest thing!

You feel like you have more, when you actually have less. Generosity changes everything.

Brian, who had his story woven into Seraphina's, had his own chapters that led to his first trip to Haiti. He has now been back five times and counting! In 2005, God used Brian's eleven-year-old daughter, Hope, to encourage him to consider a full-time job in missions. On their drive to school one morning, after they had returned from a father–daughter mission trip to Mexico, Brian was talking to his daughter about what God might have for him to do next. Hope listened for a while; then cupping her hands over her mouth and talking in a deep and slow voice, she said, "Brian. This. Is. God. Work. With. Orphans."

The trip had made a big impression on Hope. She herself had been adopted by Brian and his wife, Tracey, as an infant; and when she met the orphaned children in Mexico, she was moved. A naturally compassionate kid, she had always had a heart for the underdog, a heart that Brian and his wife had been cultivating. Since that morning ride in the car, Brian has dedicated his life to the full-time service of orphans.

As a result, Brian has now touched hundreds of orphans' lives, including the life of Seraphina, in multiple countries over these many years. And in return, their lives keep shaping his, showing him things about the Storyweaver, who always has a plan.

And Hope? She is a now high school student with

a heart that longs to rescue those who are hurting. As she puts it, "How many school kids are there in my everyday life who feel 'orphaned' or 'left out'? It's my desire to befriend as many as I can while I am here."

Sometimes giving to others means sharing something tangible, like a granola bar or a glass of clean water. Other times it's about sacrificing our time or our energy. And sometimes it's about letting go of what makes us comfortable and stepping out into unknown territory.

In chapter 3 you met Ibrahim, who walked a long way to seek help for his sick mother. You might be tempted to give credit for the happy ending of that story to the American pastor who left his home and followed God's leading to bring clean water to Africa. But he would be quick to tell you, the story-weaving in Nigeria started almost a hundred years earlier . . .

When the well-drilling team got to Nigeria in 2008, the chief of the tribe (which numbers 250,000) was given the task of choosing a specific village for the first well. He had so many options! He chose the village where Ibrahim lived because it had deep historical and spiritual roots for the tribe. It was there, in the early 1920s, that a twenty-five-year-old missionary from Michigan named Hazel Ryckman came to bring the good news of Jesus to the Rukuba tribe. She served both in word and deed, eventually starting a small clinic and school.

She traveled such a long way from her home in America. On boats, by carriage, and finally on foot. No e-mail, no cell phones, no contact with anyone she knew and loved. Why would this young woman move so far from home?

Because the Storyweaver had whispered for her to go. And she trusted his voice and stepped out into unknown territory, into the story he was writing just for her.

The chief of the tribe had been practically raised by this woman. Other key leaders of the tribe had heard the gospel for the first time from her. Hazel's impact on these people had been so great, they wanted to honor her service by giving the first well to the village that had been her home and the center of her ministry. To bring life-giving water where she had brought the message of the Living Water.

The pastor, the one who had the dream and traveled to the country to watch the first well being drilled, returned from his trip to Nigeria and researched the life of this former missionary. He wanted to know more of her story. He found online, from a rare-books collector, two letters she had written to her church, asking for support.

The letters said, "Words fail me when I try to tell you of the hopeless condition of these people. May God burden your hearts for the Rukubas, it is my prayer. In every direction thousands are dying in their sins. Four Christians in a whole tribe of about thirty thousand . . ."

When she wrote those words, she must have been so discouraged—she couldn't see any fruit for all of her sacrifice, no good seemed to be coming from all the work she was doing. But the Storyweaver was looking at more than just the page she was on, and she was given encouragement to continue. And continue she did, planting seeds, and serving for forty more years in Nigeria.

What she couldn't see then is how her story

impacted the lives of those she encountered. How more than twenty years after her death, the burden she had for the Rukubas would be felt by a church with big dreams, and how that church would bring relief to the whole village where she had lived, and to a boy who loved his mother. But not only that, the seeds of faith that Hazel planted had grown and branched out and touched the life of the doctor who treated Endurance, the life of Endurance herself, the lives of her "sisters," the life of Ibrahim's mother, and the life of the boy who lay under a rock at night and asked God to move.

If you feel that God is asking you to serve him, it's important to remember not to count on looking around and seeing evidence that you are making a difference. No matter what happens, our focus has to stay on Jesus, the one who can see what our work will mean long after we have left the scene. Hazel's story is an encouragement to me, and I hope it is to you as well. She can now see in whole what she could only see in part while on this earth. And as part of the "great cloud of witnesses" in Heaven, I'm sure she is cheering you on—excited to see what God will do with a new generation.

It's tempting when we read these stories to see "The End." But the Storyweaver is just beginning.

Just look at the lives of Divya and Christiana. No one who passed the dirty, mute woman begging on the street would ever have thought she could be used by God for anything—much less to reach out to others!

There are at least 30 million orphans in India. The Indian culture is a complicated one, where systems of class based on birth, family, money, career, gender, physical health, and religion have been in place for thousands of years.

Sometimes even those of us who have been overlooked or undervalued by such systems find ourselves trapped in a mind-set that places value on people based on what they do, or how much they have. In chapter 4, Christiana, a baby rescued from rags and educated to a position of authority, discovered that sometimes you don't have to travel far from home—from who you are or where you live or who

your family is—to do great things or have a powerful impact on your world. Christiana felt that her "escape" would be found in an important job with a good salary. But the Storyweaver had a surprise in mind for her. He had a position of influence designed just for her, right in the home where she had first come as a baby wrapped in rags.

And before Christiana was even born, Father John had been reaching out in those slums—helping others, working hard, and creating a safe place where those who were neglected, abandoned, abused, and forgotten could come and find rest. But he was just one in a long line of servants of God in India.

Amy Wilson Carmichael (1867–1951) was a missionary to India, serving for fifty-five years. She saw value in the lives others had thrown away. She even rescued children who were going to be offered as sacrifices to Hindu temples.

Amy Carmichael opened an orphanage and

REMEMBER THIS

Every story you read in this book has chapters that came before it and chapters that have come since. Your life is the same! No part you play is too small. Our job is just to be involved; it is God who makes it all come together. God is the one who changes lives. The gospel isn't about what we can do; it's about what God's already done for us! We just get to tell stories and live in stories that share this truth—the truth that . . . no one is forgotten.

"Don't let anyone look down on you because you are young, but set an example for the believers in speech, in life, in love, in faith and in purity."
—1 Timothy 4:12

founded a mission in Dohnavur. She wrote many books about her life and work in India, and about the hundreds of children who called her Amma (mother). She was a tireless servant of the Storyweaver, who never stopped seeing "the least of these" as precious, to her and to God. Her life and the way that she interacted with the people she served has influenced the work of many missionaries since, drawing them to help rescue the forgotten children of the world.

But you don't have to travel overseas to begin serving others. As Father John sat on his bench and looked out over his city, so we can look around our communities and join in his prayer: *This is your story, today and every day. Write me in it wherever and however you will.*

We are just getting started! There are 196 countries in the world, 7 billion people, and stories going on and being woven together absolutely everywhere.

You have stories from your school, your family, and your neighborhood. Imagine all the stories we have yet to see unfold! Don't wait until you are older, or bigger, or have more money or more power. Your story is unfolding today, even as you read these words. Don't miss one day of your adventure!

Interior photos: p. 10 Courtesy of Beth Guckenberger; p. 16 Copyright © Robyn Jay; pp. 12, 22, 26, 33, 47, 59, 62, 64, 67, 72, 93, 121, 132, 147, 150, 156, 161, 169, 171, 172, 174, 180, 183, 186, 196, 199, 200, 203 Courtesy of Back2Back Ministries photo archives; pp. 49, 58 Copyright © Brian Bertke; pp. 81, 86, 106 Copyright © Zach Nachazel; pp. 98, 100, 113 Copyright © Chelsie Puterbaugh; p. 109 Copyright © Chris Ramos; pp. 118, 148, 190 Copyright © Marcelle Olivier; pp. 137, 145 Copyright © Casey Foreman.

ABOUT THIS AUTHOR

Beth wrote her first book in third grade. It was about a frog. Mrs. Pate may never have liked it, but her mother still takes it out and looks at it occasionally. Since then, Beth has written other books, such as *Reckless Faith* (Zondervan, 2008) and *Relentless Hope* (Standard Publishing, 2011.)

Beth has a houseful of kids—there are some in elementary, a couple in junior high, a high schooler, a few college students, and two who live independently now. Besides her family, Beth likes all forms of chocolate, the ocean in any season, traveling, and Christmastime.

Beth met her husband, Todd, at age seventeen at a Young Life Bible study. She knew she liked him when he offered her one of his three versions of the Bible (since she had forgotten hers). Together they live in Monterrey, Mexico, where they invite you and your family to visit anytime.

Beth was kind enough to answer a few questions to help us get to know her better. If you have more questions for Beth, ask your parents for permission to send your questions to her at:

beth@bethguckenberger.com

When did you get started writing? How old were you?

I remember writing my first story in third grade. It was about a frog. I was a big reader and so had a story line (or two) always running around in my head. Today I look for stories everywhere—in movies, books, conversations, experiences . . . I want to see the story, live a good story for each day, and communicate stories every chance I get.

What were your favorite books when you were a kid?

I loved adventure stories, especially true ones, although I am a big fan of fiction. I liked funny, quirky characters and stories with resolution. I read anything I could get my hands on.

What are some of your favorite books now?

I always have a stack going on—some fiction for when I want to relax, some titles to help me understand new research in the field I serve, some biographies for inspiration, some titles given me by guests . . . The list goes on.

How long does it take you to write a book?

It depends. This one came together quickly, in several months. However, I have another title that I've been working on for more than two years. Sometimes they just need to simmer a bit, to make sure they are saying what I really think/feel. I don't need a big chunk of time to write. I can write for fifteen minutes at a time, and I often make a note with a thought or a verse or a story and then pick it up later. With a full household and a busy lifestyle, I wouldn't ever complete anything if I needed big blocks of time!

What helps you when you are writing?

Besides Diet Coke and dark chocolate? I write on a laptop, so I like to be someplace where I'm comfortable (like in my rooftop garden or on my bed), but I can write on an airplane or at a Starbucks or on a desk, if I need to. I pray, listen to music, and ask Jesus to lead. Sometimes I finish, and I don't like what I wrote or how it sounds. But even if it was just an exercise and not something that gets printed, it helps me understand what I don't want to say, and that gets me closer to what I want to share.

I've read that you have a big family. How did you end up with so many children?

It simply was how God unfolded our story. Some children were born to us, we adopted some, and some adopted us. I never imagined my family or life like this, but I wouldn't change a thing.

What kinds of stories do you like to tell your kids?

True ones. I am always telling them about someone I met or a true story I heard. I am always making them watch those tear-jerking YouTube videos that inspire people. I want them to hear (and I want to be reminded) that absolutely nothing is impossible.

What's your favorite Bible story and why?

The story in Matthew 18:12 about the shepherd and his hundred sheep. One gets lost. The shepherd isn't satisfied with ninety-nine out of a hundred, but instead leaves the ninety-nine in order to "go after the one." Every orphan I have ever met has spent his or her lifetime feeling like "the one" separated from the party of the ninety-nine. And they are wondering if anyone is coming after them.

What do you like most about being a full-time missionary? What is the hardest part?

What I like most is waking up feeling like an agent of God's mission on earth. I love the purpose it provides to my calendar and to-do lists. I love the travel and the constant feeling of being in over my head. I love watching God's hand move. I love watching someone "wake up" to his promises. I love the investment in people and in God's kingdom. I also love living in community with others who share a common goal.

The hardest part by far is being away from friends and family.

What do you like to do when you are not writing? What do you do for fun?

Hmm . . . I like good conversations, being outside, eating out. I like exercise and reading and movies and anything involving my family. I like new adventures. I try to eat or drink something new every day. I like listening to new songs and learning new words in a foreign language. I have a hunger for life and want to enjoy the day I am in, and whoever is with me in it.

What advice would you give to beginning writers?

Don't worry about the audience, who is going to read it—just write to express yourself. It should be more about communicating and connecting with others than performance. Then let people read it and ask for their feedback. Not just "Do you like it?" but "What part did you like the best?" "What was confusing?" "What else do you want to see?"

Collaboration makes everything better.

What do you think makes a good story?

Great characters, great courage or faith, and an ending you want to retell to others . . . over and over and over again.

Acknowledgments

Thank you, Ruby, Craig, Brian, Courtney, Corrie, Casey, and Dave Workman for helping me with the stories and curriculum.

Thank you to the Standard team—Dale, Laura, Lindsay, Lu Ann, Ruth, Carla, Scott, Mark, and Bob—for all you did to bring this project to life.

Thank you, Diane, for always believing in the next chapter.

Thank you, B2B community, for sharing your stories and lives with us. Love serving alongside you.

Thank you, Mom, for always trusting in the Storyweaver's plan for my life and modeling for me to do the same.

Thank you, Emma, Evan, Josh and Aidan, Carolina, Lupita, Olga, Marlen, Marilin, and Meme—every story is better with you in it.

Thank you, Todd. It's breathtaking to me how supportive you are. Cannot imagine anything better than pages lived out with you.

Thank you, Jesus, our Storyweaver—I can't wait to keep reading!

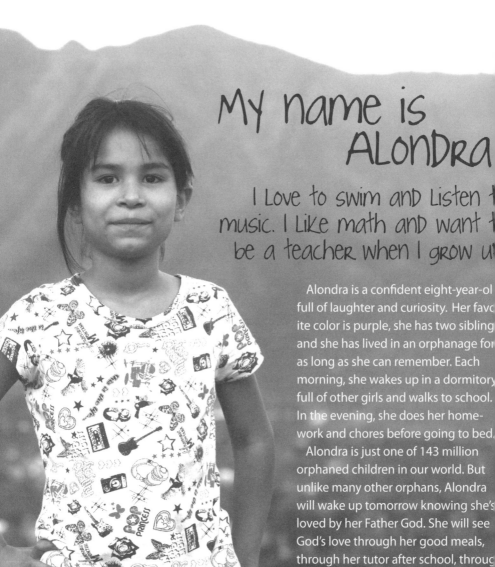

My name is ALONDRA

I love to swim and Listen t
music. I like math and want t
be a teacher when I grow u

Alondra is a confident eight-year-ol
full of laughter and curiosity. Her favo
ite color is purple, she has two sibling
and she has lived in an orphanage for
as long as she can remember. Each
morning, she wakes up in a dormitory
full of other girls and walks to school.
In the evening, she does her homework and chores before going to bed.

Alondra is just one of 143 million
orphaned children in our world. But
unlike many other orphans, Alondra
will wake up tomorrow knowing she's
loved by her Father God. She will see
God's love through her good meals,
through her tutor after school, throug
her houseparents who care for her
daily, through the visiting families wh
come to play with her, and through th
Back2Back staff who hold her hand at
church. Alondra may be physically
orphaned, but she is wonderfully loved

BACK 2 BACK MINISTRIES

want to Learn how to make a Difference?
Ask your parents to help you learn more about the orphans Beth
Guckenberger and her team serve by visiting www.back2back.org.

Back2Back Ministries • 513.754.0300 • P.O. Box 70, Mason, OH 45040

My name is Daniel.

I like to play soccer and climb the rocks behind my house. My favorite subject is English.

Daniel lives in Jos, Nigeria, where he attends Back2Back's Education Center. At the center, he has good meals, care when he is sick, and a safe place to learn.

When Daniel first came to the Education Center, he was very shy. He rarely laughed or smiled. But now, through the love and attention of Back2Back staff, he has grown to become a confident boy, full of laughter and joy.

Daniel hopes to be a teacher when he grows up. For the first time in his life, Daniel is thriving and well on his way to reaching his goals for a brighter tomorrow.

Want to learn how to make a difference?

Ask your parents to help you learn more about the orphans Beth Guckenberger and her team serve by visiting www.back2back.org.

Back2Back Ministries • 513.754.0300 • P.O. Box 70, Mason, OH 45040

Six sessions.
Four countries.
Millions of stories . . .
For Parents, Teachers,
and Leaders

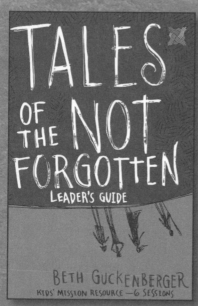

BETH GUCKENBERGER
KIDS' MISSION RESOURCE—6 SESSIONS

978-0-7847-3527-5

Want a dynamic children's missions resource? Help your kids connect their lives with the stories of children around the world!

Designed to go with *Tales of the Not Forgotten*, this six-session, customizable and interactive leader's guide (provided on CD-ROM) will help you walk kids through difficult issues—including the basic needs of children living in poverty—and lead them to find their own answers to these challenging questions:

How do I pray?
What can I give?
Where can I go?
Who will I serve?

Filled with fun activities, compelling stories, biblical teaching, and practical applications, the *Tales of the Not Forgotten Leader's Guide* will spark an interest in your students to consider God as their Storyweaver and to wonder about a world bigger than the one they know.

Visit your local Christian supplier or find it online at www.standardpub.com.

Standard®
PUBLISHING
Bringing The Word to Life